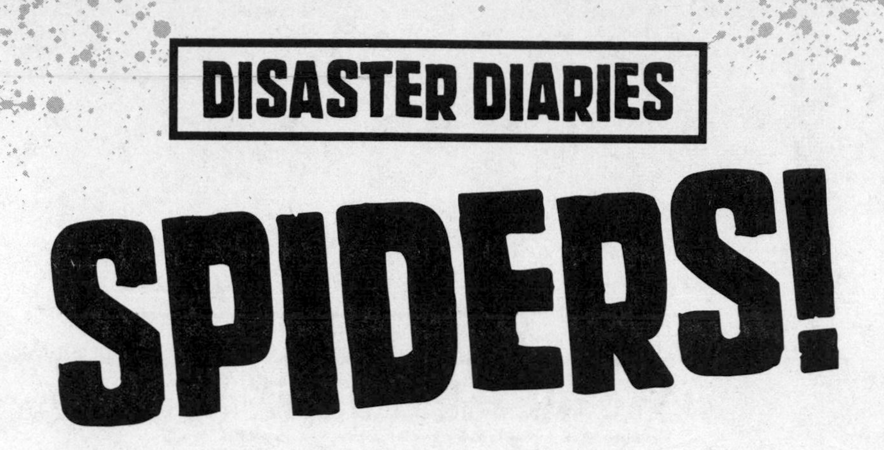
DISASTER DIARIES
SPIDERS!

DISASTER DIARIES

Zombies!

Aliens!

Brainwashed!

Robots!

Spiders!

R. McGEDDON

Imprint
MAKE YOUR MARK
NEW YORK

Special thanks to Jonny Leighton

[Imprint]
MAKE YOUR MARK

A part of Macmillan Publishing Group, LLC
175 Fifth Avenue, New York, NY 10010

Library of Congress Cataloging-in-Publication Data is available.
ISBN 978-1-250-13565-0 (hardcover) / ISBN 978-1-250-13564-3 (ebook)

Our books may be purchased in bulk for promotional, educational, or business use. Please contact your local bookseller or the Macmillan Corporate and Premium Sales Department at (800) 221-7945 ext. 5442 or by e-mail at MacmillanSpecialMarkets@macmillan.com.

Imprint logo designed by Amanda Spielman

First edition, 2017

10 9 8 7 6 5 4 3 2 1

mackids.com

Beware the turning of the page.
Inside the margins spiders lay
With poison fangs and legs so sticky,
Getting free proves rather tricky!

FOR JACKSON . . .

CHAPTER ONE

Sitting Duck was quiet.

I mean, really quiet. Like, have you ever heard a mouse play the drums? No? Well, that's because they're incredibly quiet. They just can't get a proper grip on the drumsticks and they only have tiny little arms, so . . .

Yep. They're quiet.

However, Sitting Duck was even quieter than that. And that was unusual. Because despite Sitting Duck being a boring kind of place, with seriously boring events like the world's largest stare-into-space competition and the watching-paint-dry Olympics taking place every four weeks, some really unusual things had happened.

First there were the zombies. You know, dead people with bad skin coming back to gnaw people's faces in a not-very-friendly way? Then it was the aliens, who were trigger-happy and smelled like a butt blast mixed with a cabbage burp. And then came the evil scientist and the giant robot, both of which made quite a *lot* of noise. So, without all those things destroying the town, things were pretty quiet, let me tell you.

Although, things do tend to change quite quickly in Sitting Duck. For instance:

"Dull, dull, dull!" a voice cried, shattering the quiet. It was as if someone had heard what I was writing and decided to prove me wrong; it sliced the air like a knife through a balloon. And it wasn't just a voice. If you look closely, you'll see that the voice was actually attached to a real-life person.

Hitching up his backpack, Sam Saunders came wandering around the corner. Sam was an all-out good guy and floppy-haired hero champion. Up until recently he'd been saving Sitting Duck from all the noisy threats that came its way *and* leading the town with his general kick-butt nature in the face of danger. But ever since it got quiet—not so much.

"Dull is a good thing," his friend Arty Dorkins said, walking alongside him.

"Yeah," said Emmie Lane, his other best pal. "It wasn't dull recently when we nearly got our heads blown off by a superintelligent robot." She raised an eyebrow in Arty's direction.

"For the love of dogs," said Arty. "Anyone could have made a maniacal robot bent on destruction. It was an honest mistake!"

Emmie grumbled under her breath. She was pretty sure that only big-brained Arty could do something as dumb as that. (To be honest—and I like being honest—I'm on her side. Emmie is tough, and I don't want to argue with her because she will definitely win.)

Sam remembered how fun it was fighting off the killer robot and sighed. They were on the way to school, and there was definitely nothing to be excited about there. As they made their way through Sitting Duck, the sun shining down and the smell of wet paint drifting through the air from this month's paint-drying competition, they passed the main square. Sam looked up and sighed again.

"I want to be more like him," he said, staring at a statue on top of a tall column.

"Really?" Emmie asked. "Made of stone and covered in pigeon poo?"

"Because that can be arranged . . . ," Arty added.

"No!" Sam cried. "Don't you know who that is?"

He pointed up at the statue. It depicted a man on top of a galloping horse, staring out into the distance. He wore a wide-brimmed hat set at a jaunty angle and had a crooked smile that made him look like he was about to tell a joke. He thrust out a sword with one hand, and in the other he held a duck proudly to his chest.

"Armitage Caruthers!" Sam gasped. "The greatest Sitting Ducker ever to live. They say he sailed the seven seas looking for a place to call home—fighting pirates, gorillas, mermaids—all

so he could create our amazing town!"

Arty and Emmie looked at each other and frowned.

"Mermaids?" Emmie asked.

"Yes! Mermaids are evil."

(Just for the record, I can confirm that that's true. I've met one. He stole my lunch money and spent it on tuna. In general, a good rule of thumb is that if it has scales but also talks to you, it's not friendly.)

"Anyway," Sam continued, "the point is, Armitage Caruthers wasn't afraid of *anything.* Not. One. Thing. Just like me. *And* he was always having adventures. When he eventually landed here, he took his trusty duck companion, Albertus, down from his shoulder"—he couldn't afford a parrot—"and sat him on the ground. And thus, Sitting Duck was born!"

Armitage Caruthers Character Profile

1. Born in England in Ye Olde Days (a specific historical time period of about 400 years ago).

2. Developed a reputation for adventuring when he single-handedly beat the Loch Ness monster in arm wrestling.

3. Showed a flair for piracy early on when he made his brother Barnabus walk the plank for stealing his favorite pair of socks.

4. Earned a reputation for disaster in 1666 when he accidentally left his oven on and started a small fire that burned down half of London.

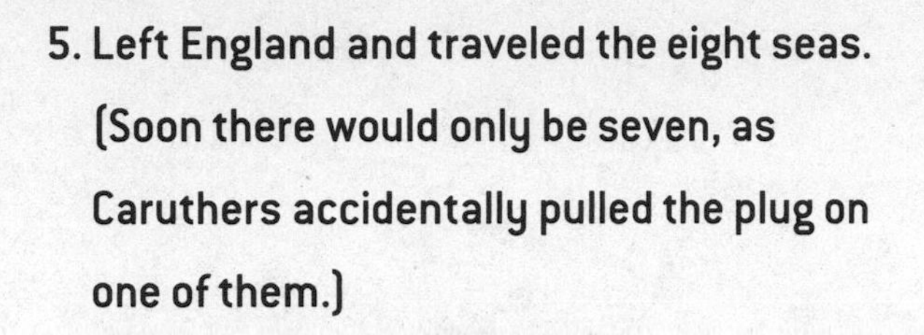

5. Left England and traveled the eight seas. (Soon there would only be seven, as Caruthers accidentally pulled the plug on one of them.)

6. Was cursed and imprisoned by the Mermaid Queen for impersonating a monkfish, but escaped and set off for the mystical New World.

7. Founded Sitting Duck but never did shake the Mermaid Queen's curse. (I told you they were evil.)

8. Died a hero, defending the town against its first catastrophic event—the Great Octopus Invasion of 1675.

9. Lives on forever in the hearts and minds of Sitting Duckers.

Sam had become so carried away with his story that his arms were flailing wildly. Arty and Emmie just let him carry on being dramatic—it really was best that way.

". . . So I'm determined to have more fearless adventures," Sam concluded as they approached the school gates. He'd managed to keep up his speech about Armitage Caruthers all the way there, and Arty and Emmie were actually relieved to see the school building looming up ahead.

As the three friends piled into the bustling main corridor, Sam's hero sensors pinged into action, and he thought he was finally going to get his chance for adventure. A strange, gloopy figure peered out from behind one of the lockers. Its eyes bugged out as if on sticks behind thick metal goggles and its hair stuck out in all directions at once, like a spilled plate of spaghetti.

"Guys, look!" Sam cried. "It's a zombie! Or, actually, an alien? Or an alien zombie?!"

"No, it's neither . . . ," Emmie began, but it was too late. Sam barreled past her and dodged through the crowd of kids. He yanked a fire extinguisher off the wall and was just about to blast that sucker into next week when . . .

"Mr. Saunders, is that you?"

A suddenly familiar figure pulled off his glasses and looked down his rather long nose at Sam.

"Oh, Mr. Nerdgoober," Sam said, gingerly putting down the fire extinguisher. "It's you." Their science teacher was often mistaken for some sort of alien creature. (Something to do with the hair and googly eyes . . . imagine, that!)

"Of course it's me," Mr. Nerdgoober said sternly. "Now come along. Class is about to begin."

Sam trudged into the classroom, disappointed he didn't get to have even a tiny bit of adventure. Arty and Emmie followed him, scurrying over to the back row, where they always sat. In front of them sat Emmie's nemesis, Phoebe, along with her friend Felicia, who was newly arrived from Silver

Spoon Academy just down the road. Their heads were bent close together as they talked excitedly about the upcoming school dance.

". . . And there'll be, like, boys and makeup and dancing . . ." Phoebe began, swooshing her hair around as she spoke.

". . . And lights and music and a fog machine," Felicia continued, her eyes sparkling.

"And I'll vomit if I have to hear one more mention of this stupid dance," Emmie finished. She wasn't a fan of dances and getting all dressed up and things like that, and she wasn't afraid to let everyone know. Felicia and Phoebe just rolled their eyes in her direction.

"That's enough," Mr. Nerdgoober snapped, desperately hoping the children would pay attention to him for once. "If you'd care to listen for five minutes, you'd hear that I have a very special announcement."

Yeah, right, Sam thought. *Unless you're really a swamp monster from Mars, I don't want to hear it, pal. . . .*

"First as you know, this term we'll be studying insects, arachnids, and all things creepy crawly. It's going to be oodles of fun! And, to make things even more fun, we'll be going on an exciting trip to the Sitting Duck Insectarium," he said.

A few murmurs of approval went up throughout the class. Sam, however, stayed silent. He lifted his head from the desk, eyes widening and heart beating slightly faster than usual.

"And second," Mr. Nerdgoober continued, "I'd like to introduce you to our new class pet, Gerry."

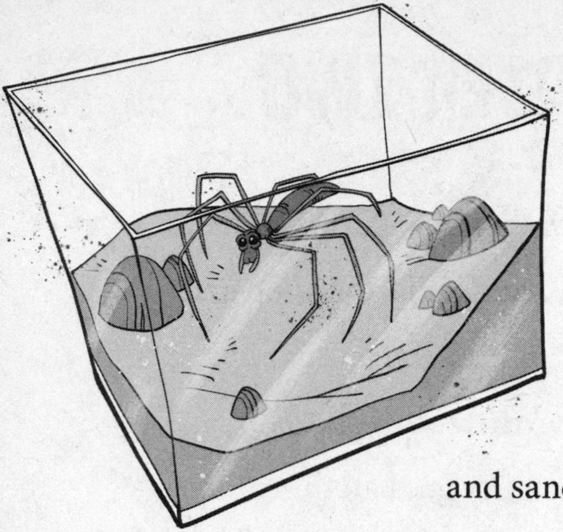

The science teacher lifted a sheet covering a rectangular glass tank. In it were some rocks and sand, but also a huge, brown eight-legged monstrosity.

"It's an ogre-faced spider," Mr. Nerdgoober beamed. "Isn't he great?"

At this, Sam turned milky white and sweat started dripping from his brow.

"S-s-s-spi-spi . . . ," he stuttered. But before he could finish, he slithered down the side of the table and landed with a thud on the cool, hard floor.

CHAPTER TWO

Emmie clutched her sides and danced up and down. She let out a belly laugh that sent a sound like a hamster in a washing machine reverberating through the hallway. Believe me when I say, that's not a fun sound. I still think of Mr. Nibbles every time I do the laundry. Well, not every time—it's been a while now. But *sometimes* I think of poor Mr. Nibbles when I do the laundry.

"Spiders?" she laughed, accidentally spitting out a bit of her lunch and a couple of quarters she'd been hiding

behind her teeth for safekeeping. "Not zombies or aliens or evil scientists . . . it's spiders you're scared of? What would Armitage Caruthers say to that?"

Arty nudged her in the ribs with his pointy elbow. "Quit it, Emmie," he said, snatching up the quarters and wiping away the gunk on his sleeve.

"Hey, give those back," Emmie cried, grabbing at Arty and quickly rehiding the quarters: one in the mound of curly hair on top of her head, the other in her left ear. "I may need them."

Sam still looked like he'd seen a ghost. His eyes were puffy like an angry cloud and his hands were jittery like a dancing wombat. Mr. Nerdgoober had tried to send him to the school nurse when he came around, but Sam wasn't having any of it. As he went to grab some books from his locker, he dropped them all over the floor and slammed his locker shut in annoyance.

"Even Superman has kryptonite, okay?" he began. "It's fine, as long as I don't have to go anywhere near Gerry, or any other sp-sp—"

"Spider?" Emmie laughed.

"What? Where?" Sam jumped, sending the books he'd just picked up flying once again. He glared at Emmie.

Arty cleared his throat and reminded Sam about the bad news. "Lots of people have arachnophobia," he said. "I'm pretty sure even Spider-Man is not one hundred percent into them. But you do know you're going to have to go to the Insectarium with the rest of the class tomorrow, right?"

Sam stood up straight and puffed out his chest and did his best to look unconcerned. "Yes. Of course," he began, "but, you know, maybe we won't go. Maybe it will be closed. Or, er, a meteor might hit it. Or maybe it will get swallowed by a sinkhole and all the spiders in the world will die a fiery and horrible death. . . ."

Emmie grinned a wicked grin. "Uh-huhh," she said slowly.

"Anyway, at least I'm not scared of this," Sam said, ambling over to a poster on the wall advertising the school dance in four days. Emmie's face creased and her fists clenched as she looked at the poster. It showed a couple of kids looking way too excited to be the only ones on the dance floor under a glitter ball. Fog drifted across the background, and the kids grinned at

each other. If I were the romantic sort, I'd say it looked quite delightful. But I'm not. So, I won't.

"I'm not scared of that," Emmie huffed. "You'd just never ever see me in a dress. I'm not like Phoebe Bowles or that weirdo new girl."

At the sound of "new girl," Arty's ears pricked up like a cactus. It was really quite a sight; I mean, his ears even *looked* sharp.

"About Felicia," he began, "you don't think she'll be going do you?"

All at once, Arty realized his mistake. Emmie began pretend-waltzing around him, making kissing noises with her lips like a wet seal landing on a damp rock.

"Mwahhh! Mwahhh! Oh, Felicia, how I love thee . . . ," she chortled.

"It's not like that!" Arty protested. "I just . . . I was just . . ."

"When can we get married?" Emmie joked. "I didn't know true love until I saw your beautiful face!"

Arty cheeks went as red as a traffic light, and he began to protest. Luckily for him, the school bell went off like an angry cat and the corridor began filling up with kids jostling in and out, forcing Emmie to abandon her merciless teasing. The three of them were about to head to their next class when Arty realized he'd left his pencil case back in the science lab.

"Shoot," he said. "I'll catch up to you guys."

"Sure thing, Romeo," Emmie called.

Arty frowned and fought his way through the packed crowd and back to the lab. He couldn't help thinking about what Emmie had said. I mean, sure, Felicia Forrester had lovely shiny hair and a big smile with all her teeth still intact. She also had two legs, two arms, and as far as he could tell was a functioning human girl with no signs of zombieism or alienness. But that didn't mean he was in lurrrrrve, right? Well, my friendly readers, let's see.

Arty pushed open the heavy lab doors and almost toppled over when he saw who was in the room. It was none other than Felicia Forrester, with her lovely hair and functioning-human-being-ness, crouched over a Bunsen burner and petri dish. Fancy that.

"Ablughadurf," he flubbed. "Heloofawah."

Felicia looked up from the bench. “Er, hello?” she said.

“Th-that’s it,” Arty said, coming to his senses. “I knew it was something like that.”

Arty quickly gathered himself and made his way over, mumbling about having left his pencil case behind. He grabbed it off the desk, wondering what in Sitting Duck Felicia was doing with all that experimenty equipment.

“Er, I’m Arty by the way,” he said, peering down at a test tube full of neon-blue liquid.

“I computed that already,” Felicia beamed, giving Arty a warm smile and shaking her lovely hair all around her shoulders. Honestly, it was so shiny it looked like a mirror. She was also so smart that she sounded like she was puking an encyclopedia.

How to Make a Good First Impression

Do:

- Use your mouth to form complex vocal noises called "words."
- Make a banana shape with your teeth and mouth, also known as a "smile."
- Shower person with candy and flowers and, if very desperate, puppies.

Don't:

- Walk in on your hands, humming the theme song from *Jaws*.
- Do an impression of a Chihuahua on a tightrope to break the ice.
- Tell them all about the warty nubbin growing on the end of your big toe.

"What you up to?"

Felicia turned away from her beakers and flasks and metal rods and flashed a wry smile.

"I'm just helping Mr. Nerdgoober out," she said. "We didn't have much science equipment back at Silver Spoon, so now I want to make up for lost time. I'm developing a growth supplement; it's going to help keep Gerry the spider in top condition. Here, hand me that beaker. . . ."

Felicia continued to explain as Arty leaned over the bench and handed her the bright green powder she requested. Apparently Silver Spoon was all about arts and drama and rainbows, but Felicia wanted to be a scientist and all she cared about were bugs and insects and animals. So, her parents moved her to Sitting Duck. No harm in that, right? I mean, it's not like a scientist in Sitting Duck has ever caused a problem before.

Felicia poured the powder into a flask containing sloppy blue goo, and turned up the heat on the Bunsen burner. At first, nothing happened, but then sparks started flying, the mixture turned yellowy-orange, and foam starting gurgling over the top of the flask.

"By the ghost of Einstein!" Felicia cried, gathering up the liquid in a set of vials, making sure not to miss a drop. "It worked!"

Arty stared in amazement. "What is that stuff?" he gasped.

"Oh, you know," Felicia began, "it's simply the molecular ionized sub-protein of a multitudinous array of benign atoms and radioactive quark compounds bound with the essence of sunshine and two crushed walnuts."

Arty—the brainiest of all Sitting Duck residents and recent creator of artificial intelligence in the form of CHARLES the robot—stared in confusion.

"It's just a little growth serum," Felicia said. "Nothing to worry about."

"S-sure," Arty stammered. Although really, the serum was the least of his worries. This girl had everything: shiny hair, all her teeth, and a brain the size of a planet.

Arty was in lurrrrrve.

CHAPTER THREE

The huge bus chugged to a stop, and the doors opened with an angry hiss. There was silence for one beautiful moment—then came the kids, stampeding for the exit.

"Everybody off!" the bus driver cried.

Hordes of children rushed through the narrow gangway and out into the parking lot. Mr. Nerdgoober followed, clutching his clipboard and flapping about like a puzzled pigeon trying to solve a math problem. Ahead of them loomed the Sitting Duck Insectarium, which, despite being full of teeny-tiny insects, was actually quite large. It looked like a giant termite mound made out of fancy steel and glass.

The students assembled outside, and Mr.

Nerdgoober hastily took roll just in case someone had fallen out the bus window on the trip. Sadly, he'd lost many students that way. Mr. Nerdgoober straightened when he realized something was wrong.

"Sam?" he called. "Sam Saunders?"

Emmie and Arty looked at each other. They were sure he'd followed them off the bus—but for a horrible moment they thought maybe he'd gone out the window instead.

"Er, we'll get him," Emmie said. "Just a minute."

Emmie and Arty piled back onto the bus and looked around.

"Where is he?" Arty hissed.

They checked behind the seats, but there was no one to be seen.

"Where did he—" Emmie began, but before she could finish a Sam-shaped thing dropped out of the overhead storage compartment and landed on her head. Strangely, the Sam-shaped thing was actually just a backpack and an old blanket someone had shoved up there. But then another Sam-shaped thing fell down as well. This time it was our trusty hero and regular spider scaredy-cat, Sam Saunders. He looked up at Emmie and Arty and an embarrassed grin spread across his face.

"Oh, hello there," he said. "Funny to see you here. I was just . . ."

"Just what," Emmie demanded, "flying a kite? Knitting a sock? Looking for the lost city of Atlantis?"

"Er. The last one?" he suggested hopefully.

"You were hiding, you big wimp," Emmie replied.

At this Sam perked right up and dusted himself off. "I am not a wimp. I am perfectly capable of getting off this bus and going to the Insectarium."

Sam, determined to prove Emmie wrong, snatched up his things and trudged off the bus, defiantly making his way toward all the other kids. Unfortunately for Sam, though, just as he approached the building he spotted something outside. It had eight hairy legs and glassy black eyes and a face that said "I'm gonna chew you up and eat you for dinner."

"Tarantula!" he cried. "We're all doomed. DOOMED I tell you!"

Arty and Emmie held him back as he tried to dash back onto the bus.

"It's just a sculpture, Sam," Arty said. "Chill."

Sam looked again at the giant arachnid. On second glance, he could see that it was made from metal and wood, and that the shiny black of its eyes was painted on. Sweat dripped from his brow and he didn't look very chilled, but he *did* accept that the twelve-foot tarantula towering over them wasn't about to eat them after all. Still, it was just as well that the tour guide and Insectarium official came out to meet them, and swiftly guided them indoors.

"Welcome, welcome, to Sitting Duck Insectarium!" the man cried as he ushered the children into the main hall. "I'm Professor Stix."

Sam looked him up and down. If there was ever a genetic hybrid between a creepy crawly and a human, this guy would be the result.

"Today, I'm going to show you the wonders of

the bug world. From the six-legged critters that make up the insects to hardy little crustaceans and eight-legged arachnids."

"Can't wait," Sam murmured.

"That's the spirit, young man. Now follow me!"

Professor Stix bundled everyone down through the glassy atrium and into the dark corridors that housed the insects. He wore a bright white lab coat and carried a walking stick that he thwacked against the ground with every pace. It was like being given a tour by Willy Wonka. (That's if Willy Wonka had had thousands and thousands of lethal bugs at his disposal, instead of delicious candy and a funny way with words.)

"Now," Stix began, "let's start with something exciting!" He rounded a corner and hurried the kids along with him. When everyone was ready, he indulged in a little fanfare, making a funny trumpeting noise with his fist and mouth, before introducing them to the notorious black widow spider.

"Isn't it something?" he gasped.

Sam peered closer, nervously. Inside the tank was a small-bodied spider with shiny black legs and a bright red spot on its abdomen.

"The red spot warns you that it's dangerous, see?" Professor Stix said excitedly.

"Oh yeah?" said Emmie. "What happens if it bites you?"

At this, Felicia cut in, desperate to show off her spider knowledge. "It causes swelling, nausea, stomach cramps, and sometimes death," she said, beaming.

Professor Stix gave her a wide smile and a thumbs-up. He seemed to think death-by-spider wasn't too bad a way to go.

"That's very clever, Miss, er—"

"Forrester. Felicia Forrester," she said.

"And I've also made this." She fished out a vial from her backpack and gave him some of the insect food. Professor Stix beamed in delight at having such an attentive student.

"Urgh," Emmie groaned. "What a show-off, right, Sam? It's not like he's going to use it."

Sam just looked around nervously, eyes darting from left to right, sweat dripping down his brow. He looked like he was in one of Arty's favorite comics, *Spiders from Space, Vol. 17: the Legs of Doom*, and he was the unfortunate victim.

Professor Stix quickly moved on to the next exhibit and unveiled to the class the tiny golden orb-weaver spider.

". . . and this specimen has some of the stickiest silk known to mankind," he enthused. "Stickier than a stick stuck to a sock!"

Spiders in Space

Speaking of *Spiders from Space*, if you've never heard of the Insects in Unusual Places franchise, you really ought to get down to your nearest comic-book store fast. Anyway, here are Arty's top-three *essential* horror comics:

- ***Spiders from Space: In Your Face***: Ah, where it all began. Featuring the gas giant guzzler spider from Jupiter, which burst out of its victim's chest and wreaked havoc on the *Starship Supernova* until a plucky heroine chopped off its legs with a sword.
- ***Bees in Your Knees***: What's that buzzing noise? Is it a bird with an alarm clock? An airplane with a faulty engine? Or is it a bee in your knee? Seriously. It might be a bee in your knee. If this comic taught me anything, it's to check your knees regularly.

- ***Praying Mantis in the City of Atlantis***: This one's a tearjerker—you just don't know who to root for. Sadly, since there is no city of Atlantis anymore, I think we all know what happens. That's right, the praying mantis chops off everyone's head and sinks the city. It's fairly upsetting.

The children didn't even blink—I mean, really, what kind of attempt at a joke is that? I could do better in my sleep. In fact, one time I told a joke in my dream and I woke up laughing in real life. It was *that* good. But anyway, I'm getting distracted, which is exactly what happened to Professor Stix and the rest of the class. Just as they moved on to the next exhibit, Felicia grabbed Arty's arm and pulled him back. She hadn't even noticed Stix's terrible joke, instead her eyes were wide with amazement.

"What are you doing?" Arty hissed.

"This," Felicia said sweetly. When she was sure no one was looking, she unlocked the glass box and thrust her arm in. "I need one for an experiment. Help me hold the lid open."

Now, Arty was a good lad, and he'd never normally be involved in such a terrible thing as stealing. But sometimes when you're a bit in love, it's difficult to see straight. Instead, you see left and right and upside down at the same time. So, as you can imagine, things get very confusing.

"Help me!" Felicia gasped as the heavy lid closed itself on her arm. Arty, love-struck and silly, propped it up, and Felicia managed to slither her hand out.

"Gotcha!" she said, bundling the golden orb weaver into a box she'd dug out from her backpack.

Arty's mind whirred and his stomach flipped a little as he wondered what he'd just done. Felicia didn't seem to care that she'd just stolen a rare specimen from the Insectarium.

He didn't have long to worry about it, though—suddenly he heard a scream from up ahead, one that he recognized. They raced to catch up and found Sam tearing around the room. Professor Stix was holding on to a tarantula, encouraging him to do the same.

"But it won't hurt you, Mr. Saunders," he said. "They're very friendly."

But Sam didn't listen and tore from the room, straight out the museum's front door. "Doomed, I tell you . . . doooooooomed!"

CHAPTER FOUR

Sam trudged out of the school building the next day and into the yard. Ever since the Insectarium, he'd been in a bad mood. He was supposed to be the hero champion of Sitting Duck, and now he was the boy who was scared of stupid arachnids. Even Lunch Lady Susan with the hairy lip had noticed how miserable he was and heaped an extra pile of boiled turnip on his plate. Obviously, stinky turnip just made things worse.

Arty and Emmie followed him into the yard, talking furiously.

"Sam, wait up," Emmie cried. "I have an idea. I think I know how to cure you."

Sam stopped dead in his tracks. "Are you serious?"

"No way," Arty said. "You can't cure someone of a phobia, not something like this."

"Oh yeah?" Emmie snorted. "Wanna bet?"

Arty puffed out his chest defiantly. "Sure! What terms?"

Emmie wrinkled her brow and tried to think of something devilish. I probably would have gone for money or power or maybe asked Arty for a unicorn that shoots candy out of its horn (if anyone could create one, it'd be Arty), but no, not Emmie.

"If you win, I'll go to the dance. *In a dress*," she declared.

Sam and Arty smirked in disbelief. They hadn't seen Emmie in a dress *ever*.

"But if *I* win," Emmie continued, "it's *you* that has to wear the dress."

Arty rubbed his chin and thought about it for a nanosecond. The possibility of seeing Emmie in a dress was too good to pass up.

"Agreed!" he cried.

Emmie spat on her hand and shoved it out in front of her. Arty reluctantly did the same and shook her slimy hand. The bet was sealed.

"Eww, guys," Sam began, but Emmie silenced him. She wasn't going to waste any time proving

Arty wrong and curing Sam. Her plan was to try to get Sam used to spiders so he didn't panic every time he saw one.

She dug around in her backpack, pulled out a plastic box, and held it up toward Sam, who peered at it curiously.

"First, I just want you to take a look," she said calmly.

Sam peered closer at the plastic box. He could just about make out a shadow darting about inside.

"Is that what I think it is?" he asked warily.

"Yup," Emmie continued. "See, it's no problem, right?"

Sam nodded and crept a little closer. Emmie, encouraged, went one step further. She lifted the lid on the plastic box and let Sam see inside. The tiny spider stood still and looked kind of cute. Its big eyes stared up at Sam as he watched it. For a split second, Sam let his guard down and thought that maybe spiders weren't so bad after all. Maybe this one was like a cartoon version of a spider. Maybe it would sing a song and help him with his chores.

"See," Emmie said to Arty triumphantly. "Easy peasy!"

"Yeah?" Arty asked. "I wouldn't be so sure about that."

Suddenly, the tiny spider began to move. First, it roamed about the bottom of the box, and then it began crawling all over the sides. Sam became very jittery and flittery, and before they knew it, he was tearing off across the school field.

"Yarhg flabba raddahh," he screamed as he pushed his way past the kids playing soccer. "Abloog a hurumph."

Arty rolled his eyes at Emmie, gloating silently.

"Okay," Emmie sighed, "that didn't work. But I'm not giving up!" She turned and ran after Sam.

Once Emmie had gone, Arty's thoughts soon

Common Phobias Dos and Don'ts

The Dark:

- Do carry a flashlight with you at all times, even outside in bright daylight, just in case the sun explodes and we're stuck in perpetual night.

- Don't enter dark caves, haunted forests, or your older brother's dingy stink lair of a bedroom.

Heights:

- Do avoid tall buildings, trees, people over ten feet tall, and birds that might swoop you off the ground and dangle you in the air.

- Don't panic. Heights are not your enemy. It's hitting the ground with your face that's the problem.

Sharks:

- Do pat sharks on the head and gently stroke their teeth in a friendly greeting.

- Wait a second . . . Scratch that.

turned to Felicia. She was basically the perfect girl, except she'd gotten him mixed up in stealing a golden orb weaver and he didn't feel great about that. In fact, it felt as if there was a snake in his stomach, like the time Mrs. Withers from Pets and Jets Animal and Airplane Supplies accidentally ate that boa constrictor. She thought it was a Twizzler and, well, the rest is history. By which I mean she's dead. Very dead.

Arty decided he was going to confront Felicia, and so he headed where he knew he'd find her: the lab.

He dashed inside—as fast as Arty dashes anywhere—and made his way up to the second-floor classroom, passing Mr. Nerdgoober, who was feeding Gerry the ogre-faced spider a pipette full of Felicia's magic formula.

"You looking for Ms. Forrester, Arty?" he asked. "She's just through there."

Mr. Nerdgoober pointed toward the antechamber next to the classroom, where most of the experiments were carried out. Arty thanked him and made his way in.

He found Felicia in a frenzy. Her lovely hair was wild and her eyes looked like they were going to pop from her head. Even her white, perfect teeth were chattering, and she was whirling around the room like a mini-tornado.

"Arty! I've done it!" she cried. "I've done it! In your face, Darwin!"

"Done what?" he called. "I wanted to talk to you because—"

"The supplement. The bug food," she continued, ignoring Arty. "I never thought it would have this effect. I mean, I hoped. I always hoped. But now it's come to pass! The molecular quark protein bonded with the spider's natural DNA radiance cells, and it must have been the walnuts and the sunshine that really did it, which is frankly a stroke of genius, because . . ."

Felicia went on for some time like this. I'm just going to let you imagine it, because it's all very scientific, and she does like to brag a bit. There's no need to give this too much book space, you know? Especially once you see what happens next.

"But what does that *mean*?" Arty asked finally, when Felicia decided she really must take a breath.

"This!" Felicia said. She moved over to the corner of the room where a sheet draped over what looked like a glass tank. With a flourish, she lifted off the sheet and revealed what she'd been talking about.

"Ta-da!"

In the tank sat Felicia's golden orb weaver, the very one that she'd stolen. Except now it was different. Very different. It had grown to humongous proportions. Its black-and-yellow legs strained against the glass—which was making cracking noises, by the way—and its body heaved up and down. Felicia had created the biggest spider the world had ever seen. No, maybe even the biggest spider the universe had ever seen (outside of the *Spiders from Space* comics, obviously).

"I don't believe it," Arty gasped. "That's genius . . . that's incredible . . . that's . . ."

"That's science!" Felicia beamed. "I'm going to

be a famous scientist! And rich, probably, because that's what comes next, right?"

"But wait," Arty said. "What happens if that thing gets out of there?"

"Oh well, what's it going to do? Take over the world?"

Arty let out a shaky little laugh. Sitting Duck did have a history of bad things like that happening. It wasn't completely out of the question. I mean, really, Felicia shouldn't jinx it like that.

Before he could reply, he heard glass shatter from the room next door, and a terrifying scream rang out.

Arty sighed. *The people of Sitting Duck just never learn, do they?* he thought. And once more, he prepared himself to meet something terrible. . . .

CHAPTER FIVE

Arty and Felicia surged out of the lab and into the main classroom.

"Uh-oh," said Arty, "that's not good."

"Not good" was pretty much the understatement of forever. At the other side of the classroom, glass lay strewn across the floor where the tank had shattered; Mr. Nerdgoober was struggling to believe what was in front of him.

The class's pet ogre-faced spider had burst out of his tank and was now towering over the poor teacher. Gerry was now almost the height of the ceiling, and from what Arty could tell from his face, he wasn't very happy. His fangs snapped together menacingly, and the two big eyes on the front of his head danced like hypnotic whirlpools. Mr. Nerdgoober seemed unable to look away.

Arty and Felicia made to go forward, but the spider let out a low hiss. He had spotted them out of the corner of one of his other six eyes—if eyes have corners, which I'm pretty sure they do.

"Wh-what on Earth?" Mr. Nerdgoober stammered as the giant spider edged closer.

"Well, it's very simple," Felicia began to explain. "I just had to split the genetic—"

"I don't think he means that!" Arty cried. "We have to help him."

Gerry edged forward, one leg at a time, until Mr. Nerdgoober was pinned to the back wall of the classroom.

"Oh, right," Felicia said. "Well, whatever you

do," she shouted to the teacher, "don't make any sharp movements."

Right then, Mr. Nerdgoober made a sharp movement.

He ducked under one of the spider's spindly legs, dashed for the whiteboard, and grabbed a pen and chucked it at the spider. It whacked him right in the face.

"Yeah, he shouldn't have done that," said Felicia.

The ogre-faced spider crouched down low and let out a rumbling hiss. Then Gerry did something terrifying.

I'll give you a moment to prepare yourself.

Are you ready?

Here we go.

Rearing up on his back legs, Gerry began producing silk from his silk glands (yeah, I told you) and rubbed it together between his front two legs, creating a kind of net.

"Wh-what's he doing?" Mr. Nerdgoober asked pitifully. But to be honest, he didn't want to know. No one would want to know what the ogre-faced spider was going to do next. Arty and Felicia knew, though. They knew all about this particular spider, and they knew it wasn't going to be pretty.

With a flick of its forelegs, the spider cast the net through the air. The force of the assault flung Mr. Nerdgoober backward, and he landed smack against the wall, pinned down by the sticky web. Mr. Nerdgoober's eyes widened as Gerry finished his attack. He towered over Mr. Nerdgoober, and in one quick movement, bit his head clean off.

Arty and Felicia stared, mouths agape.

"He really was in over his head!" Felicia joked.

"*Not now!*" Arty exclaimed, horrified. "I think we might want to get out of here."

"Yeah, good idea, brainiac," Felicia shot back.

Arty grabbed Felicia's arm and made a run for it across the classroom. But Gerry wasn't done with them yet. His head whipped around, and he used his *many* legs to skitter across the room in their direction.

Arty squared up to the beast and swung his fist. It clattered against the spider's leg and bounced back. He looked at Felicia and shrugged. "Sam usually knows what to do in this situation," he said. "Although something tells me that fighting spiders isn't going to be his strength."

Gerry towered over him, and a strand of spider spittle snaked its way out of his mouth and dropped on Arty's head.

"EWWW, GROSS!"

"Quick!" Felicia said. "This way."

She pulled Arty down and together they scurried under a desk. Gerry let out a piercing hiss that shook the windows in their frames.

Yesterday Arty would've given several teeth and maybe even his collection of rare misshapen coins that he kept in a secret vault in his bedroom to be this close to Felicia. Now he wasn't sure. To his left, there was a maniacal eight-eyed monster that wanted to bite his head off. To his right was a maniacal two-eyed child genius that was quite relaxed about creating giant spiders that could clearly kill everybody.

His chances of survival weren't looking good.

Gerry stopped scuffling around for a second, so Arty used the chance to stick his head out.

"I think the coast is cle—" he began. But before he could finish, the ogre-faced spider loomed in front of him and snorted his bad spider breath right in his face. Bad manners, frankly, but then that's a giant spider for you.

"Yargh!" he yelled to Felicia. "This way!"

Together, Arty and Felicia scuttled under the classroom's desks like the creepy crawly they were fleeing. They could hear the spider overhead, hissing and climbing over the tables.

"Now!" Arty shouted. "This is our chance!"

With that, Arty and Felicia lunged for the final desk and made for the exit. Arty whirled around and slammed the door after them just in time. A crunching noise tore through the air; Arty had taken off one of the spider's legs when he closed the door. He looked back through the glass at the very annoyed spider and silently prayed that Gerry didn't know how to open doors. Otherwise, they'd be in big trouble.

"Felicia? What in the name of all that's holey—like socks, underwear, cheese, a net—is going on?"

"Look," she began, "I didn't know *exactly* what would happen when I did the experiment, but that's the whole point of an experiment, right?"

"Mr. Nerdgoober lost his head!" Arty cried.

"I know, but he probably wasn't using it anyway, right?" Felicia tried weakly.

Arty paced the floor, his brow creased into zigzag lines.

"The Insectarium," he thought out loud. "You

gave the mixture to Professor Stix. What if he used it?"

Felicia shrugged and tossed back her hair. "Well, in terms of credit for my discovery, the scientific treaty of Monte Carlo would dictate that—"

"Never mind the Monte Carlo treaty!" Arty screeched. "This isn't about credit. This is level-one Sitting Duck trouble. We've got to act fast."

Arty looked around. There had to be something he could do. Suddenly, he remembered. Since the wave of zombies and aliens and evil scientists and evil robots, Sitting Duck had finally gotten its butt in gear and developed a warning system. Or at least the school had.

He tore through the corridor looking for the alarm.

"Aha!" he cried when he reached a bright red box on the wall. Behind a tiny pane of glass there was a black button that read:

PRESS IN CASE OF IMMINENT DOOM.
(MONDAY MORNINGS AND LATE HOMEWORK DO NOT COUNT AS IMMINENT DOOM.)

"Is this really necessary?" Felicia asked curiously. She really was taking recent events in stride.

"Oh, yes," said Arty. "This is necessary."

Arty squared his shoulders and puffed out his chest. He didn't exactly have the strongest muscles, or the most powerful punch, or, well, okay, Arty wasn't much use when it came to anything remotely athletic. But when it came to saving Sitting Duck in front of the girl he lurrrved, he was ready. Arty swung hard with his fist. The pane cracked, and he felt the button crunch. In a flash, an earsplitting alarm rang out, and several colorful, whirring lights lit up the corridor.

Arty shouted as loud as he could:

"School's out!"

CHAPTER SIX

Emmie huffed and puffed and eventually came to a stop by Old Branchy, the ancient tree in the far corner of the school playing fields. Armitage Caruthers, the buccaneering town founder, coined the imaginative name. To be honest, back when he named it, it was probably a Young Branchy, so I don't really know what he was thinking.

Below the tree sat Sam, trying not to shake like a leaf. He looked up at Emmie with a grim smile.

"Sorry about that," he said. "I did *try* not to be scared."

Emmie was about to say something sarcastic and snippy as usual, but instead she decided to cut Sam some slack. Occasionally she could be nice like that. Like that one time her great-aunt Doris's cat, Attila, didn't try to claw her eyes out when she came within twenty feet.

"That's okay," she said, then immediately reverted to her normal self. "But I really don't want to have to wear a scratchy dress, so it would be helpful if you could get over it soon, okay?"

Sam just nodded glumly. He looked up into the sky and wondered whether he was ever going to get his hero status back. As if on cue, his ears picked up a shrill ringing traveling on the breeze from across the fields. It grew louder and louder until, in a flash, it became a roar. He and Emmie looked back at the school and saw lines of children and teachers streaming out of the building and running in different directions.

"What's going on?" Emmie asked. "Did Big Stan the Doughnut Man come around again?"

Sam peered back at the school. He couldn't see any sign of Stan. And even though his doughnuts were amazing, he didn't think that the school alarm would be going off because of it. Something much more exciting must be going on.

Sam sprang to his feet and darted across the field. "C'mon, Emmie," he said eagerly, "let's go!"

The two of them made their way back to the school, where the throng of kids and teachers whirled around in a panic. Sam made his way toward the main doors, a smile on his face, sure he was about to put his heroism to the test.

Suddenly, he felt a tug on his collar and turned to face the looming presence of Lunch Lady Susan.

"You can't go back in there," she yelled. "There could be fire or explosions or danger of all sorts!"

"Why?" Emmie asked. "Did one of your turnips go up in smoke?"

Emmie flinched under Lunch Lady Susan's gaze, and Sam squirmed in her grip. She had muscles like a sailor and the mustache to match. He'd have to think his way out of this one.

"Look!" he cried. "Zombie!"

"Argh!" Lunch Lady Susan squawked. "Protect the turnips!"

In her panic, she loosened her grip on Sam's collar, and he twisted out of her grasp and sprinted into the crowd of people. Emmie managed to escape Lunch Lady Susan as well, and he caught sight of her doing a diving roll through the legs of Mrs. Strictheart, the meanest of the mean principals. But before Strictheart could banish her to detention, they made their way inside the school.

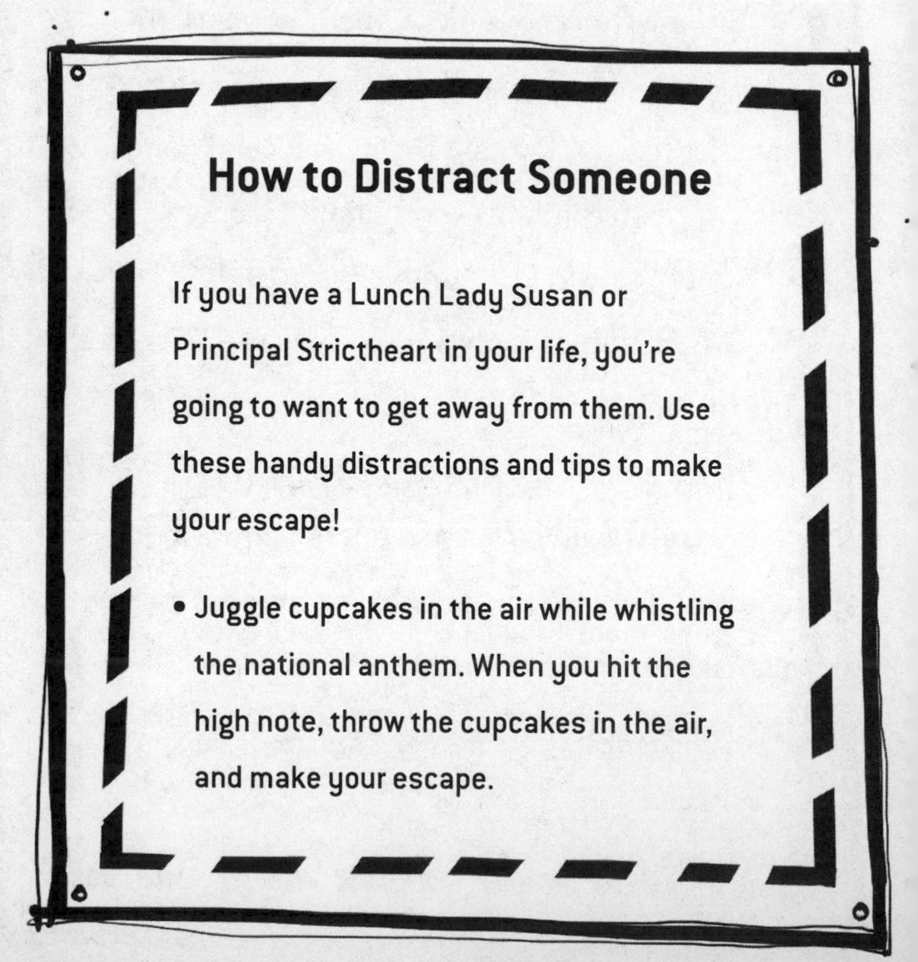

How to Distract Someone

If you have a Lunch Lady Susan or Principal Strictheart in your life, you're going to want to get away from them. Use these handy distractions and tips to make your escape!

- Juggle cupcakes in the air while whistling the national anthem. When you hit the high note, throw the cupcakes in the air, and make your escape.

- Dance the tango with an elephant to invisible music. If you can't find an elephant, look harder, they're huge! You can't miss them. Seriously. I don't think you're trying.

- Concoct an elaborate story about how all the bad presidents and queens and kings in the world are all actually just mermaids in disguise. (I'm telling you, they're evil!) Slip away while they ponder your theory.
- Give them a smartphone and open a social media app. Flee while they scroll through their feed. (Trust me, they'll be there for hours.)

The corridor was eerily deserted, but Sam and Emmie pressed forward. Sam led the way, lights flashing off and on above him and the whine of the alarm ringing loudly in his ears.

He lifted his nose into the air and sniffed: no sign of smoke. He wondered what or who had triggered the alarm. It was Thursday, so he knew it couldn't have been the anti-Monday brigade playing tricks. This time it was real.

Sam and Emmie turned the corner off the main corridor.

"Ew," Emmie cried, "what's that?"

She looked down at her foot and peeled it off the floor. Her sneaker was completely covered in some sort of sticky goo. Sam pulled out his flashlight from his backpack.

"Lemme take a look at that," he said, peering closer. Sam reached out a hand and touched the strange substance. It was like golden bubble gum, all sticky and gooey and gross.

"Do we have some alien species on our hands?" Emmie asked.

"Maybe," said Sam, puzzled.

He and Emmie continued down the corridor.

As they turned past the science labs, Sam put a hand on the wall to steady himself . . . and touched the exact same goo that Emmie had stepped in.

A thought flashed across his mind.

"Does this remind you of something?" he asked, his blood turning icy in his veins.

"Well," Emmie said, "Arty does have a booger problem, but I didn't want to say—"

"No, not that." Sam could hardly bring himself to speak. "I was thinking more like, sp-sp-spiderwebs."

"A-ha-ha-ha," Emmie laughed, slapping Sam on the back. "Don't be ridiculous. A spider like that would be gigantic. Something beyond the realms of imagination. Something that could only happen in your nightmares, Sam, or in a *Spiders from Space* comic. Something that could only exist if the apocalypse struck and—"

A droplet of golden goo dripped down between them. Sam shone his flashlight at it, scattering golden light across the hall. He craned his neck upward and saw something that made the blood drain from his face.

Felicia's golden orb weaver had grown even bigger, and it had obviously escaped its glass tank. And apparently it had learned how to open doors.

"It's not possible," Sam gasped in horror. But it *was* possible, very possible. The golden orb weaver was hanging from the ceiling, clacking its fangs like the hungry menace it was. Slowly, it lowered itself down and stood in front of them on its eight gangly legs. With a high-pitched squeal and a

click of its fangs, it lunged at Sam and Emmie.

"Yargh!" they screamed in unison. Their legs motored and their arms pumped as they desperately flung themselves through the school corridors and away from the spider. Sam was so used to fleeing from spiders that he tore through the school like an Olympic sprinter on rocket boosters. Emmie wasn't so lucky, though, and soon lagged behind.

As they skidded around a corner, Emmie lost her footing and went tumbling head over butt. The golden orb weaver loomed over her, the spider's mouth spread in what looked like a grin.

"Sam!" she cried. But it was no use. Sam was a gibbering wreck.

Emmie dug around in her backpack and found her own flashlight. She flung it at the golden orb weaver, and it landed on one of its eyes with a thwack. The golden orb weaver hissed in fury, giving Emmie just enough time to pull herself up and drag Sam along with her.

"Let's get out of here," she yelled.

Together they barreled through the corridor. Emmie's brain went into overdrive—if they could just get to the gym, they might have a chance.

The spider was closing in on them just as Emmie charged through the gym doors. She frantically looked around and grabbed a hockey stick propped up against the wall, and pushed it through the door handles to barricade the door.

"That might have done it," she said hopefully.

Sam nodded, his top lip trembling and his hands shaking.

But their hope was short-lived.

There was a loud *BOOM* as the golden orb weaver smashed its giant head against the door. Emmie hurried forward to shore it up, but it was no use.

With a splintering crack, the door flung open and the orb weaver entered.

Emmie and Sam were trapped.

CHAPTER SEVEN

Meanwhile, across Sitting Duck, Arty and Felicia pedaled furiously on their bikes. They were on their way back to the Insectarium to raise the alarm before it was too late. At least by now the school would be evacuated, but Arty couldn't help but wonder whether Sam and Emmie were okay.

As they cycled through the gates, they saw a disturbing sight. The model tarantula outside had several legs missing, strewn across the ground like twigs. The huge glass-and-steel structure was still standing, but several windows were broken, and the whole thing looked like it had been on the wrong side of a disaster movie.

"This doesn't look good," Arty said, clambering off his bike.

"Hmm," Felicia said loftily. "It might not be what it seems."

Arty despaired. It was obviously going to take a lot to convince Felicia that a town full of marauding spiders was a bad idea.

Together, they slowly made their way inside, dodging shards

of glass on the ground. The previously bright and welcoming atrium was now dark and deserted. Light fixtures swung from the ceiling like pendulums and electric wires stuck out of the wall, sparking. Something seriously bad had happened, another disaster in Sitting Duck, just waiting to be put right. (Which keeps me in business, to be honest, so it's fine by me!)

"Stix!" Arty hissed through his teeth, trying to locate the professor. All he could hear was his own voice bouncing back at him off the walls. He pulled a flashlight out of his backpack and stared through the gloom.

"You've really done it now, Felicia," Arty said. "Stix must have fed your concoction to the whole Insectarium! He's probably toast!"

"Buttered?" she asked.

Arty sighed, exasperated.

"Look, it's all in the name of science," she explained. "Silver Spoon didn't understand, either. Just one little accident, and all of the sudden I'm a 'danger.'"

"What kind of accident?" Arty asked. "Did you get expelled?"

Felicia nodded. "I accidentally blew up half the school with sodium chloride and a handful of eggs. But I was just trying to find a cure for the common foot bunion. It was a worthy cause."

Arty nodded. Common foot bunions were one of the leading causes of death for Sitting Duck residents, just after being eaten by a zombie and blasted by an alien ray gun. But still . . .

"And then when I heard we were studying

minibeasts this semester, I wanted to try out something new."

Arty stared at her, realizing that Felicia wasn't just a lovely, genius girl who had done the odd experiment here and there; she was a serial experimenter who had left a trail of destruction behind her. He sighed. Sitting Duck was a trouble magnet. In fact, he vowed to find this trouble magnet and destroy it. Or else write a very angry letter to someone in charge, and get *them* to destroy it for him.

Arty wondered how he could've been fooled by her . . . if only he'd realized sooner what she was up to! At least he, Sam, and Emmie had some serious experience in world saving. Maybe if they were quick enough the spiders wouldn't destroy the whole planet—just some of it.

Felicia Character Profile

1. Mirrorlike hair that swooshes in the breeze
2. Emergency test tubes for last-minute experiments
3. Traveling lab in her backpack, for all experimental needs

Past Crimes:

- Blew up Silver Spoon Academy trying to cure the common foot bunion
- Blew up her parents' garage trying to isolate the gene for superintelligence . . . Ironic, huh?
- Blew up her kitchen when trying to create the "Elixir for Instant Cheer," an experimental drink that contains ¼ soda, ¼ ice cream, ¼ gummy bears, and ¼ love and friendship

1
3
2

In the meantime, though, he didn't really feel like asking Felicia to the dance anymore.

Arty tried to shake off his disappointment as he and Felicia steadily walked deeper into the Insectarium. As much as he might be annoyed at Felicia now, he knew they'd have to stick together to get through this. And anyway, she got him into this mess; maybe she could get him out.

A shriek shook Arty out of his reverie. "Children! Help!"

A terrifying scene appeared in the gloom. A gigantic eight-legged freak had Professor Stix pinned to the wall like a living poster. Its body was black like the night, shiny, and glistening. Its pincers clicked back and forth threateningly, and its body swelled like a balloon behind its head.

Arty and Felicia recognized the bright red splotch on its abdomen instantly. There was only one spider it could be.

"Black widow!" they murmured, looking at each other in alarm. If they didn't do something fast, Professor Stix was finished.

Arty summoned up his courage and barreled toward the giant black widow. Felicia tried to call him back, but he knew it was now or never. With all his force, he leaped onto the black widow's giant balloon-like body and shunted the creature off to the side. It let out a shriek as its legs crumbled beneath it and it slumped against the floor.

"Take that, you toxic bugbrain," he called. "No more web of evil from you!"

Sam was the one who usually did the cool put-downs at the moment of triumph, but he wasn't there, so Arty had to say *something* to sound all cool and hero-like. I don't think Arty did too badly, actually, but I have heard better action-hero quips.

Arty and Felicia grabbed Professor Stix and pulled him to his feet. He looked like he'd seen a ghost, or a giant six-foot spider that was about to kill him, which in fact he had. That same giant six-foot spider was also getting to its feet, though, and this time it was *really* mad.

"Look out!" Felicia cried. The black widow's pincers bit down, clutching Professor Stix's shoulder. Quickly, he squirmed out of his lab coat just as the toxic venom seared through his coat like acid.

Arty realized they didn't have a chance to outrun the spider; it was fast and vicious and would be on them in a second. He looked around for a weapon—and found the perfect thing. Dodging the black widow, he yanked the fire extinguisher off the wall and threw it as hard as he could back to Felicia. It rolled under the black widow toward her.

Felicia pointed the fire extinguisher straight at the spider. For a moment, she hesitated—this was a giant black widow after all, a boon for science. But then she realized that having another dead scientist on her hands would look bad on her Nobel Prize application.

"Eat foam, loser!" she cried. (Again, not a bad action-hero put-down for a novice, I think.) White foam surged toward the black widow. It screeched like a banshee and fumbled backward under the force of the blast.

"Now's our chance," Arty yelled. "Come on!"

Together, Arty, Felicia, and Stix raced through the corridors of the Insectarium, slamming shut as many doors as possible in their path to prevent the black widow from following them.

When it seemed safe enough, they stopped to catch their breath. Professor Stix gasped and spluttered. He couldn't understand what had happened.

"I've never seen anything like it," he said. "The black widow . . . it ballooned!"

Arty and Felicia glanced at each other. They knew exactly what had happened. Felicia happened. She began to explain that the vial of spider food might have gone a bit out of control, and while she may have started off sheepish, Arty swore he could hear a hint of pride in her voice.

"But that means—" Professor Stix began.

"What?" Arty asked.

Professor Stix ignored Arty and instead ushered him and Felicia back to the atrium where all the spider tanks had previously been. Tanks lining the walls had shattered. Glass was piled up in the middle of the room, and a giant hole in the former foyer wall opened onto the building's front lawn. The whole place looked like a mouthful of smashed teeth.

"I gave a droplet of the food to every spider in here," he said. "They must have all grown out of control, just like the black widow."

"And how many spiders were in here?" Felicia asked, starting to get a little nervous.

Professor Stix looked around. "Hundreds," he said.

Arty gulped. At this point, he should have expected it. It wasn't just the school and Insectarium that were under threat—it was the whole of Sitting Duck. Of course.

He spoke in as firm and heroic a voice as possible. "Professor Stix," he said, "alert the authorities. We're going to need everyone we can get in order to fight back against the spiders."

"And what are *we* going to do?" Felicia asked.

Arty peered around the room, a determined look set firmly on his face. "We're going to save Sitting Duck . . . and the world!"

CHAPTER EIGHT

Question: Have you ever hung upside down from a swing? Or some monkey bars? Or has your big brother ever dangled you over a pool by your ankles, taunting you until your mom and dad made him stop? Well, imagine that, but then imagine also being in a spider's web, suspended twenty feet in the air. Not fun, am I right?

Well, imagine no more. Or rather do imagine, but imagine it happening to our heroes Sam and Emmie, because that's exactly the situation they found themselves in. They were trapped, high up in the corner of the school gym, suspended in sticky golden silk with an angry-looking spider prowling around below them.

"Hey, ugly!" Emmie shouted. "Get outta here before I rip off your legs and use them as drumsticks!"

The golden orb weaver hissed back at her. I don't think it understood. I mean, it's unlikely spiders grasp the concept of playing drums—despite how awesome they'd be, what with all their legs and everything. But anyway, the spider seemed to sense that Emmie wasn't happy and decided to make its feelings known.

Emmie struggled against the bonds and looked over to Sam. His face was as white as a cloud, and his teeth were clamped together so tightly that the veins in the side of his head were throbbing. It is fairly safe to say he wasn't enjoying the experience of being stuck in a giant spider's web.

"How're you doing over there, champ?" Emmie said, grinning.

Sam glared back, eyes popping and hairs standing on end.

"That good, huh?" Emmie said. "Then I guess it's up to me."

Emmie racked her brains. What they needed was to get down from this sticky web before the spider was ready for its lunch. But before that, they needed to get it out of their way, which meant that they needed a distraction.

Emmie scanned the room for inspiration. All she could see was sports equipment scattered around and the moldy gym bag filled with centuries-old clothes for when you forgot your own. Emmie shuddered—she'd once had to wear a frilly shirt that looked like it was from the 1920s.

Her eyes caught on the high windows skirting the edge of one of the walls, and quickly she formulated a plan. Windows make for good distractions, you see. Especially when they're broken.

"Sam," she hissed, "we need to make some noise, to get that critter out of our way. I bet if we break that window, we've got a chance."

Sam looked up and nodded vaguely.

"You got a baseball with you, Sam? In your backpack?"

Sam always carried a baseball, and usually a bat. He never wanted to miss the opportunity for a quick game. Although right now, he thought there were probably more important things going on.

"I need you to smash that window," Emmie said. "Then we're getting out of here."

At the thought of "getting out of here," Sam finally snapped to it. He reached around to his backpack, which was stuck in the sticky web. He rummaged around as best he could and eventually dug out his baseball.

"And then what?" he asked. "We're still twenty feet up in the air!"

"Leave that to me, Sam," Emmie said, with a mischievous glint in her eye.

Sam shrugged and pulled back his arm. He threw the baseball as hard as he could, sending it flying through the air and straight through the windowpane.

The spider squealed in confusion. Just as Emmie expected, it barreled out of the gym to investigate the cause of the crash. Emmie pumped her fist with joy and began to put the rest of her plan to work.

She yanked her arm as hard as she could until it pulled free from the sticky web with a satisfying tearing noise. Then she rummaged around in her backpack and pulled out her trusty screwdriver. Many a time it had saved her—mostly when she was sneaking out of Great-Aunt Doris's house and needed to unscrew the door from its frame.

She hacked at the golden webbing on her legs and body with the screwdriver until she had disentangled herself from all the threads. She freed Sam, and they both clung on to the remaining web as Emmie carefully unspooled a length of the silk until it became a rope long enough to scale the perilous drop.

"You ready for this?" Emmie asked.

"You bet," said Sam. "Let's get as far away from that thing as possible!"

Together, they counted down, "Three, two, one . . ." and pushed back off the web.

"Geronimo!" Emmie shouted as she and Sam sailed through the air, hanging off their silken rope. They glided like monkeys through a jungle canopy but landed like cows on an ice rink, slamming into the hard wooden floor of the gym.

"Wow," Sam gasped, rubbing his elbow. "Let's do it again; let's do it again!"

Emmie stared at him dumbly.

"Oh right, yeah. Let's not," Sam said. "In fact, let's get out of here before that brute comes to get us."

"Agreed!" said Emmie.

With that, the two of them sprinted out of the school and into the yard. No one was there. It was like the whole of the school, teachers and all, had disappeared into thin air. Even the smell of Lunch Lady Susan's twelve-day boiled turnips seemed to be missing.

"Something weird's going on," said Emmie.

"Weirder than a giant spider prowling the school?" asked Sam, with a quirk of his eyebrow.

"Weirder than that," Emmie said, nodding. "Quick, Sam, let's see if we can get in touch with Arty."

Sam pulled out a walkie-talkie from his pack.

"**A**lpha-**R**omeo-**T**ortoise-**Y**ankee," Sam began. "This is **S**ierra-**A**lpha-**M**ango. Do you read me?" (He always introduced himself using the phonetic alphabet, to make sure he was heard loud and clear. Sadly, he also always got at least a couple of words in the phonetic alphabet wrong, but he still tried, bless him.)

There was static and then a faint reply from Arty. "**S**ierra-**A**lpha-**M**ike," he said (because

Arty always got these things right). "Under attack . . . town center . . . come quick."

The transmission fizzled out, and Sam and Emmie looked at each other, resolved. Sitting Duck was under threat and Arty needed them.

Phonetic Alphabet

If you need to be heard over the telephone or radio or some sort of new-fangled Internet talkie-gadget, the phonetic alphabet is your friend. Just spell out letters of a word you need to say, with words of their own. Like *Lima* for *L* or *X-ray* for *X*.

But if you don't want to use the normal phonetic alphabet, with its Sierras and Tangos and Papas and Hotels, there's nothing stopping you from making your own. As long as you and your pals all understand it.

You can make up what you like, like I do:

- *A* is for *Anteater* or *Acne* or *Anteaters with Acne, come quick!*
- *E* is for *Etc., Etc.*
- *L* is for *Lollipops* or *Limas* or *Lampposts*
- *O* is for *Orangutans* or *Olives* or *Ooh, hello there, I haven't seen you in a while!*
- *S* is for *Shoot, I'm running out of ideas here.*
- *T* is for *Think of your own if you're so clever.*

"Come on," Emmie yelled. "Let's go!"

Sam and Emmie grabbed their bikes from the bike shed and set off into town. Pretty soon it became apparent that things were not all good in Sitting Duck. For instance, they passed Mrs. Jones of Mrs. Jones's Phones and Loans, who was sprinting down the street, her wig flailing off the back of her head. "Run for your lives, children. The curse of Sitting Duck has struck once more!" And then came Angry Pete, who liked to sit on the corner and shout conspiracy theories at everyone in town. "I knew those spiders were against us all along!" he raged.

"What did he say? Spider*S*?" Sam exclaimed, extra-emphasizing the *s*. "I thought there was only one?"

As soon as he said it, they came upon the sight

of hundreds of spiders crawling and crushing all over the town center. Some were big; some were small. But they all had eight legs, and all were deadly.

Emmie picked up her walkie-talkie to contact Arty, but Sam stopped her.

"No time for that Emmie." He gulped. "Or we'll be **D**elta-**E**lephant-**A**lpha-***Dead***!"

CHAPTER NINE

Giant spiders came from all directions. Residents of Sitting Duck fled in all directions. Yet Sam was paralyzed with fear, rooted to the spot like a palm tree in the face of a tsunami. Emmie grabbed Sam by the wrist and yanked him closer to her so they wouldn't be separated in the whirling mass of spider bodies and legs.

"Come and get us if you dare!" she yelled defiantly, which was pretty silly, really, because she didn't have a weapon and also spiders don't understand words. If they wanted to come and get you, they pretty much would. In fact, the spiders had finished terrorizing the Sitting Duckers—most of whom were stranded in sticky webs hanging from lampposts—and decided to do just that.

"Er, on second thought," Emmie said, backing away.

Soon, she and Sam found themselves completely surrounded. Sam wielded the baseball bat he'd taken from his backpack, but his knees were knocking together and his hands were shaking.

A spider loomed in front of him with big hairy legs and a nasty gleam in all of its eight eyes. Sam cowered in fright, and Emmie puffed out her chest, ready for one last stand.

"CHARGE!" a voice cried. But it wasn't Emmie, or even Sam. (Surprise!) It was good old Arty, who swept in alongside Felicia and smacked the spider with his flashlight. "C'mon," he yelled, "follow me!"

Together, they made their way through the mass of spiders. While they searched for somewhere to hide, Arty filled them in on what was going on with Felicia, her evil experiments, and all that. Emmie seethed in fury.

"So you did this?" she barked at Felicia. "I knew I didn't like the look of you."

Felicia just pouted and turned up her nose.

She still thought she'd done a pretty cool thing, even if it did cause death and destruction and all-around panic. Nothing was going to change her mind on that one.

"Hey," said Arty, half-heartedly defending her. "It's not all bad. At least I won't have to wear a dress to the dance, will I, Sam?"

The prospect of Sam overcoming his fear of spiders anytime soon seemed pretty remote, so he just nodded in agreement. Emmie scowled. There had to be some way to help Sam overcome his fear. She really didn't want to wear a dress, either, and it would be really handy if Sam's hero powers came to the fore again, considering the almighty pickle they were in.

Quickly, before the spiders could overrun them, they scrambled up into a tree on the main square and surveyed the scene. Fires raged in one corner of Sitting Duck, and the huge Duckbill Tower that overlooked

the harbor was covered in the leggy critters. Hundreds of residents poured through the streets and across

the main square, desperately trying to evade the spiders.

"This is worse than the zombies!" Arty gasped. "At least they just wanted brains. These guys want to eat all of you!"

"Ah, those were the days," Emmie sighed. "Right now I'd take some dumb zombies or CHARLES the evil robot over these guys."

The four of them perched in the tree as the spiders rushed by. Felicia was thrilled by it all, Arty and Emmie were anxious to put things right in Sitting Duck once more, and Sam held on to the branch so tightly his knuckles turned white. Without warning, a piercing scream rang out from across the way. All four of them turned their attention to the middle of the square.

"What in the name of science—" Felicia began.

There, on his own, was Professor Stix. He was desperately clinging on to the monument in the center of the square as hundreds of spiders crowded around him, eagerly expecting a meal.

"Professor?" Arty cried. "But he was supposed to be raising the alarm!"

"I don't think he needs to raise an alarm," said Emmie. "Everyone knows by now that Sitting Duck is under attack."

Further screams went up, and the spiders hissed with glee. Any minute now, poor Professor Stix would go the same way as Mr. Nerdgoober and half the other residents of the town.

"We have to do something," Arty cried.

"Sam?" Emmie asked. "Any ideas?"

Sam mumbled a reply and looked on in panic—but Emmie wasn't having any of that.

"Sam, come on!" she cried, shaking him. "Sitting Duck needs you. What happened to the hero champ we used to know? What about the guy who wanted to be just like Armitage Caruthers: fighting the bad guys, defeating evil, and being an all-around awesome hero and Sitting Duck legend? What happened to the guy who would do anything to stop his best friend Emmie from having to parade around in a dress?"

"Hey," Arty complained. "If you don't have to, then I will!"

Emmie's speech seemed to stir something inside Sam. He looked out from the tree and caught a glimpse of old one-eyed Armitage Caruthers, proudly atop his bronze horse in the center of Sitting Duck. Once upon a time, he would've given anything to be like him, and now he was scared of a few lousy spiders. Caruthers had faced much worse—ahem, evil mermaids—and lived to tell the tale.

It was as if a light had come on in Sam's eyes. His brain's hero machinery was finally kicking into gear, like a robot getting a software upgrade. But he wasn't a robot; he was a hard-core hero champ. Sitting Duck was *his* town, and he wasn't about to let it be overrun be eight-legged freaks. He picked up his baseball bat and jumped from the tree.

"Sam," Arty cried. "What are you—"

But Sam was running and wasn't listening to Arty at all.

"For Albertus, the original Sitting Duck!" he cried, marauding his way through a crowd of hungry spiders. He raised his bat and thwacked away a hungry-looking wandering spider—its fangs clacking in anger. A jumping spider came next. It leaped to and fro, using its long legs as springs to bounce. Sam didn't hesitate for a minute. He sprang up onto a nearby bench and launched himself into the air, bringing down his bat with a satisfying crack.

"He's gone *full beast mode*," cried Emmie. "That's my boy!"

Sam continued on, bashing spiders left and right, until he reached Professor Stix. Just as Stix was about to have his head chewed off by a crazed tarantula, Sam swooped in. He dived under the tarantula and knocked out its legs from under it. The tarantula crumpled and began veering sideways like a hairy Leaning Tower of Pisa. Sam

Sam's Hero Levels

Hero Level Normal: Sam is an all-around nice guy and charming fella, witty and wisecracking and always popular with old ladies and shaggy dogs.

Hero Level Silver: The enemy approaches and Sam adopts his ready pose, waiting like a ninja to strike

Hero Level Kick-Butt: Sam channels all the rage of Sitting Duck into a powerful force and unleashes it on his enemies

Hero Level Beast Mode: Er, I've never seen this before. But I think it's gonna be good.

scrambled out of the way as its burly body crashed down onto the ground.

"Professor!" he barked. "Help has arrived! This way to safety!"

Professor Stix gratefully took Sam's hand, and together they made their way out of the square and back toward Arty, Emmie, and Felicia. Sam held Stix's hand aloft in triumph, and his smile seemed to stretch way off his face and out into the space beside him.

Arty and Emmie cheered. Sam had finally mustered up his old courage and faced his fear.

"I'm back!" He beamed. "And those spiders are dead meat!"

CHAPTER TEN

Sam, Arty, Emmie, and Felicia picked up their bicycles and made their way out of the town center. After depositing a terrified Professor Stix with the local police, they headed back toward Sam's house. Now that he was back in action, Sam was determined to save Sitting Duck once more. I for one am glad he pulled himself together. I missed Sam the hero.

Sam held on to his bike with one hand and swung his baseball bat with the other. "Yee-haw," he cried.

Arty, Emmie, and Felicia struggled to keep up. Sam was a man on a mission, swiping spiders' legs out from under them and cackling through the streets. But no matter how many spiders he stopped, there'd always be another one in its place.

"C'mon, guys," he yelled. "Let's head over to my place. We need supplies. We've gotta figure out a way to stop this thing."

When they finally made it to Sam's house, they ditched the bikes in his front garden and barreled through the front door. Sam thumped right into his dad, Mr. Saunders.

"Oh, Sam, you're just in time!" he gasped. "*Ballroom Dance Stars* is on, and I know you won't want to miss it! You might get some tips for the school dance!"

The kids stared up at him, aghast. Mr. Saunders was the mayor, supposedly in charge of keeping everyone safe and looking out for the welfare of the town.

"Err, Dad," Sam began. "The spiders?"

Mr. Saunders peeked out of the window. "Hmm, they are rather large for this time of year. Don't worry, son, they can't get you in here."

The kids just looked at one another, shaking their heads. Honestly, adults can be so silly sometimes, it's hard to believe. Good thing I'm not an adult.

Okay, I am, but least I'm one of the good ones.

"Sam senior!" came a voice from the living room. "You're going to miss the cha-cha."

Mr. Saunders did a little jig and strolled back to the living room. "Well, your loss, kids," he said. "Mind how you go with that baseball bat. You don't want to get yourself into mischief."

"Right, Dad," Sam replied, and bounded upstairs with the others. Sometimes I question the decision making of parents who would rather be watching reality TV than saving the world. But what do I know?

The kids gathered in Sam's bedroom. As always, it was down to them to save Sitting Duck.

"Are we absolutely sure we have to do something to stop the spiders?" Felicia asked. "This could be my one shot at the Nobel Prize."

Dance Moves for the End of the World

If the end of the world is nigh and you'd prefer to dance your way out of a pickle, look no further than these nifty dance moves:

- *The Despairing Owl:* Cover your face with your wings (or arms, if you have them) and rock back and forth on the nearest tall tree you can find.

- *Stealth-Fighter Shuffle:* Bounce up and down like a curious meerkat, while you scope out the landscape and the threat you face.

- *The Broken-Nose Break Dance:* Dodge your apocalyptic enemy with nifty footwork, and hit back with a spinning kick.

- *Save-the-Day Samba:* Dance to the rhythm of your sweet, sweet victory.

"Er, we definitely do need to do something!" Emmie barked. "Those things nearly had us for breakfast, lunch, and dinner!"

Sam racked his brains. The first thing they needed to do was to protect the citizens of Sitting Duck. If the adults couldn't do it, then they would have to do it for them.

"I suggest we head out into the fray," he said, "to assess the situation."

The others nodded solemnly.

"But first," he said, "we're raiding the secret stash."

Sam led them back down the stairs and through the back door. From the living room, they could hear cries of "wonderful," "magnificent performance," and "I've never seen anyone dance like that since Cinderella turned professional!" Sam ignored the "fun" his parents seemed to be having and led his team of heroes down to the shed.

He cracked open the door and peered inside with his flashlight. "Everyone grab something," he said. "We're gonna need weapons."

Emmie grabbed a four-pronged pitchfork, Arty wielded a shovel, and Felicia picked up a dainty trowel.

"What?" she said as everyone looked her way. "I'm sure it'll work just as well."

Emmie glared at her. "Your heart's not in this at all, is it?"

Sam hurried them out of the shed and out onto the streets. Night was falling in Sitting Duck, and the dusky gloom made the atmosphere a bit more terrifying. Not for me, obviously; I'm not afraid of anything. Mice maybe . . . rats . . . tall trees . . . people with rolled-up sleeves . . . saying the alphabet backward . . . mushrooms. But other than that, nothing.

The point is, on Sam's street, everything was quiet and eerie, and even the shadow of hedges in the streetlights looked like long-limbed spiders ready to pounce. Just to complete the effect, a scream pierced the night like a pin in a balloon. A man in a dingy-colored jumpsuit ran toward them at full pelt.

"Oh," said Arty. "It's Marty Hiller the Cockroach Killer. Hello, Marty!"

Emmie nudged him in the ribs. "It's not time for hellos, Arty—look!"

Behind Marty came two giant spiders. They looked like terrifying Brazilian wandering spiders. Usually, Marty was the one doing the bug killing, since he had his own pest-removal van that blitzed around town getting rid of all sorts of unwanted critters. But now it seemed that the minibeasts were getting their revenge. Funny how things turn out, am I right?

"Run, children, run!" he screamed as he pelted toward them. "The end is nigh!"

Sadly, Marty wasn't watching where he was going as he sprinted through the streets, and he smashed head-on into a lamppost. He bounced off it and staggered around, clutching his head. Sam could practically count the stars whizzing around it. He and Arty rushed toward him to help, but before they could, one of the spiders sank its fangs deep into Marty, paralyzing him with its toxic venom.

"NOO!" Arty cried, swiping at the spider with his shovel. One of the spider's legs was sliced clean off and went spinning across the street.

As Arty and Sam challenged another spider, Felicia and Emmie dealt with the one that had attacked Marty. Felicia half-heartedly threatened the spider with her trowel, which promptly knocked it out of her hand. It also knocked her off her feet, sending her back spinning across the road.

"B-b-b-but," she began as it towered over her, "I created you! Don't you know what a miracle of modern science you are?"

Just as the spider was about to clamp its fangs, it caught a scent on the air. Its legs bristled, and it moved over to where Felicia's backpack lay on the ground.

"The vial," she shouted. "It wants more feed. . . ."

Before the spider had a chance to grow any bigger or feed any more, Emmie launched herself at it with her pitchfork. She drove the blades right into its back, and it collapsed onto the ground.

"That's how it's done!" She laughed.

Meanwhile, Sam and Arty had dispatched their own spider, and they came running over to Felicia and Emmie.

"Marty is no more," Arty said sadly.

"The bugs finally beat him, did they?" Emmie said.

"Looks like it," said Sam. "But they're not going to beat us. . . ."

He surveyed the scene and pointed down the road. At the bottom of the street, Marty's van lay ripe for the picking.

". . . Because I've got an idea!"

CHAPTER ELEVEN

Sam held a flashlight between his teeth and struggled with the zipper of his jumpsuit. He, Arty, Emmie, and Felicia were safely in the back of Marty's van, and they were getting ready for bug warfare.

"Gotcha!" he cried as he zipped up the suit.

He heard a muffled cry from the other corner of the van.

"Mmfur grumpifrr kumpilow . . ."

Arty, bless him, had gotten himself stuck upside down in his suit. Emmie and Felicia yanked at it until his head finally popped out the top like a startled gopher.

"All good," he huffed, a little out of breath and his hair a lot wild.

Marty's van was a boon for bug killers like them—it was full of everything they'd need to take the spiders down for good. Once they'd suited up, they filled their backpacks with big plastic containers full of bug poison and attached metal spray nozzles. It'd be just like shooting a water gun or a flamethrower, only much more deadly.

"Eat your heart out, Ghostbusters." Sam laughed. "We're the Spiderbusters!"

Arty let out a groan. "Oh man!" he said. "My suit is on the wrong way."

So much for a hard-core band of Spiderbusters. Arty quickly rearranged his jumpsuit and tried to look as tough as possible.

Emmie was eager to get down to business. "So what's the plan, Stan?"

"The name's Sam, actually," Sam said seriously. "You should know that by now."

Emmie began to explain that it was just a saying, but Sam kept on talking.

"The plan," Sam continued, "is this . . ."

Sam guessed that the spiders were attracted to the potion Felicia had created. It must be supertasty to them, like Pop-Tarts or soda or that delightful cookie dough you're not supposed to eat raw but you do anyway. So, what they had to do was use it against them. Maybe if they could create enough of it, they could lure the spiders into one place and blast them into next week. And if they were lucky, next month.

"Er, so what's the plan?" Felicia asked.

"Oh, right, yeah," Sam said. Thing is,

he hadn't actually said what the plan was; I just explained it to you. He must have forgotten or something. Anyway, he then actually said the plan out loud and made sure the group was all on the same page of the book, as it were.

"Right!" Arty agreed. "In that case, what are we waiting for?"

Together, they jumped out of the van and back into the streets.

Sam, encountering a smaller house spider, hit it with his baseball bat, then, when it was staggering, he let rip with his spray soaker. The poison shot forth in a deadly mist and felled the spider instantly.

"Yee-haw," Sam said. "I think this plan is gonna work!"

Together, they rode through the Sitting Duck streets and back toward the school. By now it was pitch-black and the whole place was deserted. Smashed windows littered the ground where spiders had been up to no good.

"Let's make our way to the lab," Arty said. "Then we can work on the formula."

All four of them crept inside the school, which looked like the set of an apocalypse movie. Lockers were open and papers were strewn across the floor. School was definitely out.

Ahead of them in the corridor, they heard a familiar sound: the low hiss of an oncoming spider.

"Get in position," Sam yelled. "Now!"

Sam kneeled down, and Emmie stood beside him. Arty and Felicia stood on either side, ready for the takedown. Felicia finally seemed to realize that if she didn't do something about the spiders, the spiders would do something about her. By which I mean they'd eat her for breakfast, lunch, and dinner.

The spider came around the corner, the same spider that had left Sam and Emmie hanging above the gym—the same spider Sam had been terrified of not so long ago. It was the golden orb weaver.

Sam smiled. "Not today, bozo. FIRE!"

As the golden orb weaver lumbered toward them, all four of them sprayed cascades of poison, and the spider let out a piercing cry as it fell under the deluge. It scrambled about on its legs like my uncle Pete at a wedding reception, but ultimately it fell under its own weight. (Again, like my uncle Pete at a wedding reception.)

"Gotcha, you jerk!" Sam cried. "Now come on. Let's get to the lab!"

"There goes my beautiful creation," Felicia sighed.

"Don't worry," Emmie huffed. "There are plenty more where that came from."

The four of them jumped over the body of the giant spider and barreled through the corridors. Felicia tried to gather up some of the golden silk from the walls and floors, but Emmie dragged her along.

"B-but it's a souvenir," she wailed. "And it might make us rich, too!"

Emmie was having none of it: "Unless you're going to use the silk to make Arty a new dress, then we don't have time for all that," she said. "Although, that might be a good idea." She laughed, looking toward Arty. "Sam is back in action."

Arty tried to look unconcerned, but it was hard. It wasn't like he couldn't pull it off, he told himself, especially if the dress was red—he always looked good in red.

"Yeah, well . . ." He tried to think of a comeback, but had nothing.

Instead, Felicia jumped in. "I'll still dance with you, even if you have to wear a dress."

Arty blushed. Even though she was a maniacal scientist girl who created world-threatening spiders, he thought it might be quite nice to dance with Felicia. Stupid nice hair and teeth.

Finally, they made it to the lab. The windows were blasted out and the place was a mess, but it still had everything they needed. They skirted poor Mr. Nerdgoober—or what was left of him—and made their way to the benches.

Felicia and Arty got to work; Emmie slammed the door shut.

How to Make a Gigantification Potion:

Well, like Felicia said, you'll need:

- Benign atoms
- Radioactive quark compounds
- Essence of sunshine and two crushed walnuts

But you'll also need secret ingredients:

- Purified water droplets from the mystical Fountain of Youth (alternatively, water from a tap)
- One silver toenail from the mythical phoenix of Mount Mysticus
- Two electrons captured from the nearest host star (available at all good atomic supermarkets)

Simple, really!

Instead of the dainty glass beakers they had used previously, they used a giant bucket. Instead of one Bunsen burner, Arty hooked up all twenty-five of them in the classroom, making an intense flame that burned blue like an angry sea.

Sam and Emmie watched through the door's window as a whole host of giant spiders came rustling down the corridor.

"Quickly," said Sam. "We need as much as possible."

Arty and Felicia worked fast, measuring ingredients and filling up a huge container full of the spider-growth elixir, but the spiders were soon peering through the door, trying to knock it down.

"I can't hold it!" Sam gasped, barring the door with his shoulder.

"Here!" said Emmie. She ran to the nearest stool and propped it under the door handle. Hopefully it would save them some vital minutes.

Just then a *fizz* and a *pop* ripped through the room. The bucket full of growth elixir sprang into life, sending yellowy-orange goo fizzing in every direction.

"That's the stuff!" Arty cried.

With the mixture complete, it was time to get out of there.

"Guys, go!" Sam yelled, grabbing the bucket as the spiders bashed against the door once more. Emmie, Felicia, and Arty all clambered over the desks and out the broken windows, shinnying down the drainpipes to the relative safety of the outdoors.

Sam smiled at the spiders through the glass. "See ya later, suckers!" he shouted. Letting go of the door, he ran for the open window as the spiders rushed in after him. Then he leaped to freedom.

CHAPTER TWELVE

Sam, Arty, Emmie, and Felicia had a plan to put into action. While Sam and Emmie stayed at the school ready to spring a trap, Arty and Felicia would lure all of the spiders in Sitting Duck there. Right now, they were pedaling furiously around town, like a pair of rogue cowboys on wheels, to round them up. (Or should I say spiderboys? No, that doesn't quite work.)

Arty and Felicia were counting on spiders being hungry for more of the elixir. They were going to create a trail of it right from the center of Sitting Duck, back to the school, and they rode out into the center of town to corral the spiders like the Wild West.

When they reached Main Street, they stopped to review the situation.

"Right," said Arty. "Here's what we do."

He poured some of the elixir into the bikes' water bottles, making sure to store them upside down. His idea was to open them up and let the elixir fall out while they pedaled, creating a trail that would lead the spiders to the trap. He put the bottles in place and climbed off his bike to yank the lids off two garbage cans.

"Grab one of these," he said to Felicia. "You're gonna need it."

Felicia looked at it, puzzled. Arty clambered back onto his bike and held his up like a shield. "We'll need protection," he began, "when we go through *that*."

Felicia looked ahead and saw a huge mass of

spiders congregating. "Oh," she said. "Good call."

Felicia grabbed the trash-can shield in one hand and a handlebar in the other.

"You ready?" Arty asked.

Felicia nodded. She had a tear in her eye and a sigh in her heart, but she knew it was pretty much destroy the spiders or they would destroy everything else. And then how could she do experiments and go to fun school dances? Awesome giant spiders are one thing, but, you know . . . priorities!

Arty and Felicia popped their water bottles open and began pedaling.

They hit the first wave of spiders, which reared up and gnashed their jaws. Arty and Felicia fought back, batting them with their makeshift shields. They fought their way through the crowd to the top of Main Street, which joined with the town square.

"It's working, Felicia," Arty shouted. "Look!"

As the food dripped out behind them, more and more spiders raced in pursuit like the hungry bugs they were. They even abandoned the prisoners they'd captured in their sticky webs to follow Arty and Felicia.

Felicia braked sharply as a tarantula reared up ahead of her. It made to clamp down on her lovely hair with its not-so-lovely fangs, but she drew the garbage-lid shield up in front of her and brought it crashing down on the tarantula's legs. It seemed that she finally got the message: small spiders good, giant spiders bad. It reeled in pain behind her, but then picked itself up from the ground and followed her once more.

She motored on through the swarm, Arty encouraging all the way.

"That's it," Arty said. "We're nearly there."

As they rejoined the road that led up to Sitting Duck school, what followed was like a nightmarish version of the Pied Piper. Instead of leading rats or children through the town, Felicia and Arty were leading a hungry band of giant spiders to their deaths. Although actually, I'm pretty sure the Pied Piper would have approved.

Eventually, they came to the school gates and pedaled inside. They crossed the yard and went straight to the open door. They cycled down the corridors, spiders clambering after them, and headed straight for the school gym.

"I hope they're ready," Arty panted.

Oh, they were, Arty. No need to panic.

While Felicia and Arty had been pedaling around town, Sam and Emmie had gotten down to work. The school dance was supposed to take place tomorrow night, but Sam and Emmie had decided they were going to have a party of their own a little early.

Arty and Felicia frantically burst into the hall.

"Sam, Emmie, where are you?" Arty cried

as he and Felicia ditched the bikes—there was nowhere left to pedal.

"Up here!" Emmie shouted.

Arty and Felicia followed the voice until they spotted Sam and Emmie, perched halfway up the bleachers by the side of the wall. Arty and Felicia scrambled up toward them, and, panting, made it up to the final steps.

"What now?" Arty gasped.

"Now," said Sam, "we take them down."

With a flick of a switch, the gym was suddenly bathed in bright, colorful light. The disco ball that had been set up twirled in the center, sending multicolored rays spinning across the ground. The spiders, packed into the gym like the world's worst dance attendees, hissed and screeched, but now there was nowhere left to run.

The group put on the protective masks they had found in Marty's van.

"Hit it!" Emmie cried.

Sam hadn't been that keen on the idea of the school dance, but the one thing he did think was cool was the fog machine. It was supposed to be for the romantic number at the end of the night. You know, the one where everyone gets all smoochy-smoochy, and people start mashing

their faces together like seals fighting over a mackerel? Anyway, the point is, the school had a fog machine. Except it wasn't going to be used for harmless smoke this time. No. It was going to be used for bug poison. And the spiders were going to dance to their doom.

"Take that!" Sam cried, and flicked the switch. Clouds of poison from Marty's van seeped across the school hall. White smoke billowed into the eight-legged creeps, and despite their best efforts, it took them down, one by one.

Meanwhile, Felicia, Emmie, and Arty used their spray packs to fight off spiders that tried to get close to the bleachers. In a couple of minutes, the school gym was like a battlefield, and the spiders had clearly lost.

Sam gave Emmie a high five.

"We did it!" he cried.

CHAPTER THIRTEEN

Just as they were about to celebrate, one last spider came to spoil the fun. This time, it was the biggest, baddest, and meanest of them all.

"Uh-oh," said Sam. "Looks like Gerry is not too happy."

Not content with biting off poor Mr. Nerdgoober's head, Gerry the ogre-faced spider was back for more and ready to kick butt.

Our trusty heroes ran out of the school gym, where the poison from the fog machine was slowly thickening. Even with masks, they had to get some fresh air. As they burst out into the open, Gerry eagerly followed them.

"Quick!" Arty shouted. "Use your sprayers!"

Sam, Arty, Emmie, and Felicia dove into formation and tried to fire off more of the poison, but only a pathetic dribble came out of the hoses. Their weapons were empty, and Gerry was closing in for the kill.

"Quick, run!" Emmie cried. But before she could go anywhere, Gerry rubbed his front legs together and cast a net in her direction. She let out a muffled cry as the sticky web pinned her to a nearby wall.

"Emmie!" Sam cried. He and Arty rushed toward her and tried to pry her out of the sticky morass.

Gerry hissed and let out another high-pitched squeal. He rubbed his legs together again and spun more silk into a net. This time, he cast it in Sam and Arty's direction. If he were an evil villain, he would have said something like "Don't get tangled up!" But Gerry wasn't an evil supervillain; he was just your regular giant spider going about his business. And he couldn't form complex sentences or make hilarious spider-based puns.

What he could do was fling his sticky net out toward Sam and Arty. They both yelped in panic, but it was no use. The web completely covered them and pinned them to the wall alongside Emmie. Sam and Arty struggled under its sticky grip, but it was no use.

"Argh!" Arty yelled. "Get us out of here!"

Felicia was left alone against the eight-legged monster that she herself had created. She backed away from the creature as he slowly advanced toward her.

"I can't," she yelled. "The size differential between this arachnid and my humanoid frame is such that the equitable force needed to shift its—"

"Felicia!" Emmie cried. "Quit with the science chat and get us out of here."

Gerry sent a web flying in Felicia's direction. She ducked it with a squeal and rose back to her feet. Past Gerry, she noticed Sam's baseball bat lying in the road. This was her moment. This was where she got to be a heroine, instead of the dangerous science girl who created this whole mess in the first place.

She rolled between Gerry's legs and grabbed the baseball bat. Then she rose to her feet and stood firm in front Gerry's ogre-y face.

"Take this, you oversized, genetically modified, ugly-faced teacher killer!" she screamed, swinging the baseball bat right at Gerry's face. She thwacked him right on the spider nose—which, actually, is not a real nose. It's an area of hair on the spider's legs that picks up smells and transfers them to the spider's tiny brains. So, what I should have said was, Felicia thwacked the spider on the legs.

The spider groaned and toppled forward. As he fell, Felicia finished him off with a nice strike to the head, which knocked him out completely.

"You did it!" Arty cried.

Felicia raised the baseball bat in the air in triumph and danced around like she'd just scored the winning touchdown at the Super Bowl.

"Okay, yeah," said Emmie. "It's great fun watching you dance, Felicia, but is there any chance you can get us out of here?"

“Oh right,” Felicia said.

She helped Sam, Arty, and Emmie out of their gunky prison and got them back on their feet just as a whole cavalcade of police cars and fire trucks and ambulances came whirring into the school’s parking lot. Flashing lights filled the night sky and sirens blasted out into the air as the kids walked out of the gym to greet them. In the crowd, they saw the familiar car of their principal, Mrs. Strictheart.

“Kids!” someone exclaimed. They turned to see the burly chief fireman, Harlow McWaters. “We’ve come just in time. We’re here to save Sitting Duck.”

The children just looked at one another. Every. Single. *Time.* The adults really had no idea what was going on in this town. They were about as useful as a bear in a tutu—but much less hilarious.

"Oh, okay," Sam said to the fireman. "The danger's in there!" He thought it was best for the authorities to just get on with their thing. No use telling them that the whole of Sitting Duck and the world had been saved by four kids. The town's firefighters and police all piled into the Sitting Duck school, desperately attempting to solve a problem they were far too late to solve.

Mrs. Strictheart got out of her car and strode toward our heroes.

"Do you know how many science teachers we've gone through?" she asked. "We've had more of them than we've had dinners!"

The kids looked on shamefaced.

"Who is responsible for this?" she demanded.

Felicia stepped forward and offered herself up. "Me, I suppose," she began. "Is this the part where I get my Nobel Prize for scientific discovery and a special award for bravery?"

Mrs. Strictheart scowled. "No," she said curtly. "Come with me."

Arty looked on wistfully as Felicia was escorted away to yet another expulsion. He gave her a little wave, and she swooshed her hair as if to say "good-bye." It was sad, really. She'd obviously seen the error of her ways. Probably. For five minutes, at least.

Sam looked across to Arty. "No dancing for you two I'm afraid."

Arty slapped his forehead. "Don't mention the dance, you fool!"

"Hey, yeah!" said Emmie. "I almost forgot!" She rummaged around in her backpack and found just what she was looking for: a green sequined dress. *Darn it*, Arty thought, *it's not red.*

Arty reluctantly put it on over his clothes. In the flashing police lights, I think he looked quite nice.

"A bet's a bet," said Emmie.

"I guess," Arty said. "Way to get over your phobia, Sam." But he grinned.

Sam just laughed. "It was totally worth it!"

Read them all!

Disaster strikes the town of Sitting Duck again . . . and again . . . and again. . . .

DISASTER DIARIES

ROBOTS!

Read on for a sneaky look at the disaster-defeating wisdom you don't want to miss out on in this other book. . . .

Sam, Arty, and Emmie get more than they bargained for when Arty creates CHARLES for the school science fair. CHARLES is meant to be a helpful chore-completing robot, but when he malfunctions, he proves to be a maniacal droid bent on destruction—all in the name of "tidying up" the town of Sitting Duck for good.

When CHARLES raises his robot army—complete with pesky hairdryers and dangerous refrigerators—Sam, Arty, and Emmie must take on their own creation to save the town once more!

CHAPTER ONE

It was the day of the school science fair, and the eyes of the world had once more turned on the sleepy town of Sitting Duck.

Well, not the whole world, obviously. That would be silly. Everyone in the *whole world* hadn't gathered together to watch a small school science fair. They wouldn't all fit in the hall for a start, and the line for the bathrooms would have been a mile long.

In fact, if I'm honest, there were mostly just teachers and students wandering around making the place look untidy—but if you hold your school science fair in a school, what else can you expect?

Tables were lined up inside the hall, each one

displaying a different project. A lot of them were modeling-clay volcanoes that fizzed white foam out of the top when you poured vinegar in. But, in an interesting twist, one was white foam that supposedly shot vinegar out of the top when you dropped a volcano in. Although no one had thought to bring a volcano with them, so it couldn't be put to the test.

As well as all that stuff, there was one thing even more important in the school hall that day—friendship. And heroes.

Okay, that's two things.

In fact, here come a couple of those friendly heroes now: Sam Saunders and Emmie Lane.

What can I say about Sam that hasn't already been said? Well, he's probably about your height, actually, or maybe a bit smaller. Or taller.

Depends what height you are, really. He's roughly around your height—let's just say that.

Sam loves sports. Like, really loves them. Whether it's baseball, football, soccer, basketball, or dodgeball, he can't get enough of that stuff. When he's not playing sports, he's hanging out with his best friends, being liked by everyone he meets, and *saving the frickin' world*!

Emmie, I'll be honest, isn't liked by everyone. But that's fine, because she doesn't really like everyone, either. It works out quite well, actually, as it means most people try to avoid talking to her in case she shouts at them or something.

Her hobbies include being angry, plotting elaborate escapes from her great-aunt Doris's house, and leaving sarcastic comments on YouTube videos. Oh, and *saving the frickin' world*!

Sam and Emmie were strutting like a pair of champions through the hall, clutching their own science projects and checking out the competition. As they approached one table, a creature with a dozen eyes popped up from behind it and let out a high-pitched squeal. Instinctively, Emmie lunged at it, ready to wrestle the thing to the ground, but Sam caught her just in time.

"Relax," he said. "It's just Phoebe."

"Like, of course," said Phoebe. "And what do you mean 'just' Phoebe?"

Phoebe Bowles was Emmie's all-time worst enemy, and considering Emmie had recently battled a power-hungry mad scientist with a brainwashing machine, that was really saying something. Emmie was very much your average running-around, climbing-trees, punching-supervillains-in-the-face type of person, while Phoebe loved nothing more than . . . well, herself, really.

"What are you wearing?" Emmie asked, her eyes drawn to Phoebe's hat. It was a fluffy blue

beret, but sticking out from it at all angles were six metal arms. At the end of each arm dangled a little mirror, making it look like a hundred eyes were reflecting outward.

"It's a rotating mirror hat," sniffed Phoebe, like it was the most obvious thing in the world.

"What's a rotating mirror hat?" asked Sam.

"Are you kidding me?" Phoebe snorted. "It's, like, a hat with mirrors on it. So you can see yourself from every angle. It's my science project."

Sam spotted Emmie's fists clenching.

"Right!" he said. "Good luck with that."

"What have you made?" Phoebe asked. "Something lame, I bet."

Sam produced a deodorant can and sprayed it into the air. Phoebe sniffed, then immediately stumbled back, clutching her nose and mouth.

“Eww! It smells like something died!” she said, grimacing.

“Exactly,” said Sam. “It’s antizombie deodorant. One spray and you can pass yourself off as one of the living dead!”

“Why would you want to do that?” asked Phoebe.

“In case zombies ever come back,” said Sam.

Phoebe frowned. “Zombies?”

“Yeah,” said Sam. “Like last time? Remember?”

Phoebe stared blankly at him.

“Hundreds of them. Arms dropping off and stuff,” Sam continued.

Phoebe shook her head.

“You turned into one,” said Emmie. “And ate an old woman.”

"Oh, *that* time," said Phoebe. "Gotcha." She turned to Emmie, peering down her nose. "What did you make?"

Emmie held up what looked like a TV remote. "It's an alien detector."

"Aliens?" said Phoebe. "There's no such thing."

Emmie and Sam exchanged a glance.

"Yeah, well, if they ever do turn up, an alarm in this thing will go off," Emmie said.

Suddenly, the alien detector came to life, and a very loud alarm rang out. So loud, in fact, that half a dozen volcanoes erupted throughout the hall.

"Shut that

thing up!" yelped Mr. Nerdgoober, a science teacher who definitely had a bit of an alien look about him. It was his eyebrows, mostly. And his pointy ears.

Emmie whacked the device on Phoebe's table, silencing it instantly. Mr. Nerdgoober nodded curtly and then scurried past.

Sam and Emmie left Phoebe with her mirror hat and went to see Arty, the third member of their little band of hero-friends. Arty is *all about* science, so the science fair was right up his alley. If Arty had to choose between science and candy, he'd choose candy. But science would come a very close second—that's how much he loves it.

Arty had kept his project a closely guarded secret, so Sam and Emmie were intrigued when they saw the bulky shape hidden under a sheet at his table.

"Ready for the big reveal?" Arty asked, bouncing from foot to foot with excitement.

"We've been ready for weeks!" said Sam.

Arty gathered up the sheet and pulled it away with a flourish. "Ta-da!"

Sam peered closely at the hunk of metal and wires, trying to make sense of it. "Wow!" he said. "It's . . . it's . . ."

"Bits of metal junk bolted together?" asked Emmie.

"It's not junk!" Arty protested. "It's CHARLES."

At the mention of its name, the pile of definitely-not-junk whirred to life. Wires twitched and metal unfolded, until Sam and

Emmie were staring into a pair of LED eyes and a series of lights that looked like a smile.

"I am CHARLES," said the robot in a voice so cheerful it made Emmie's hair stand on end. "It stands for Chore Helper and Really Lovely Electronic Pal!"

Emmie went over the letters in her head. "Surely that would mean you were called CHARLEP?"

"I couldn't exactly call him CHARLEP, could I?" Arty said. "What sort of name's CHARLEP for a robot?"

"What does he do?" asked Sam, leaning in to get a closer look.

"Chores!" Arty said. "All that dull stuff like tidying your room, ironing your clothes, whipping up cream. You'd never have to do any of them again! And he's gonna win me this science fair!"

Just then, Mr. Nerdgoober clambered up onstage and tapped the microphone to get everyone's attention.

"Ladies and gentlemen. And children. And pets," he began. "The judges have deliberated, and it's time to announce the winner of this year's fair."

"This is it." Arty beamed. "The greatest moment of my life . . ."

"With a fantastic entry sure to inspire generations of scientists to come, it's Miss Phoebe Bowles and her miraculous rotating mirror hat!"

A squeal went up from behind them, and Phoebe made her way to the podium. A steady smatter of applause filled the hall.

"Still the greatest moment of your life?" Emmie asked.

"No," Arty replied. "This is the worst!"

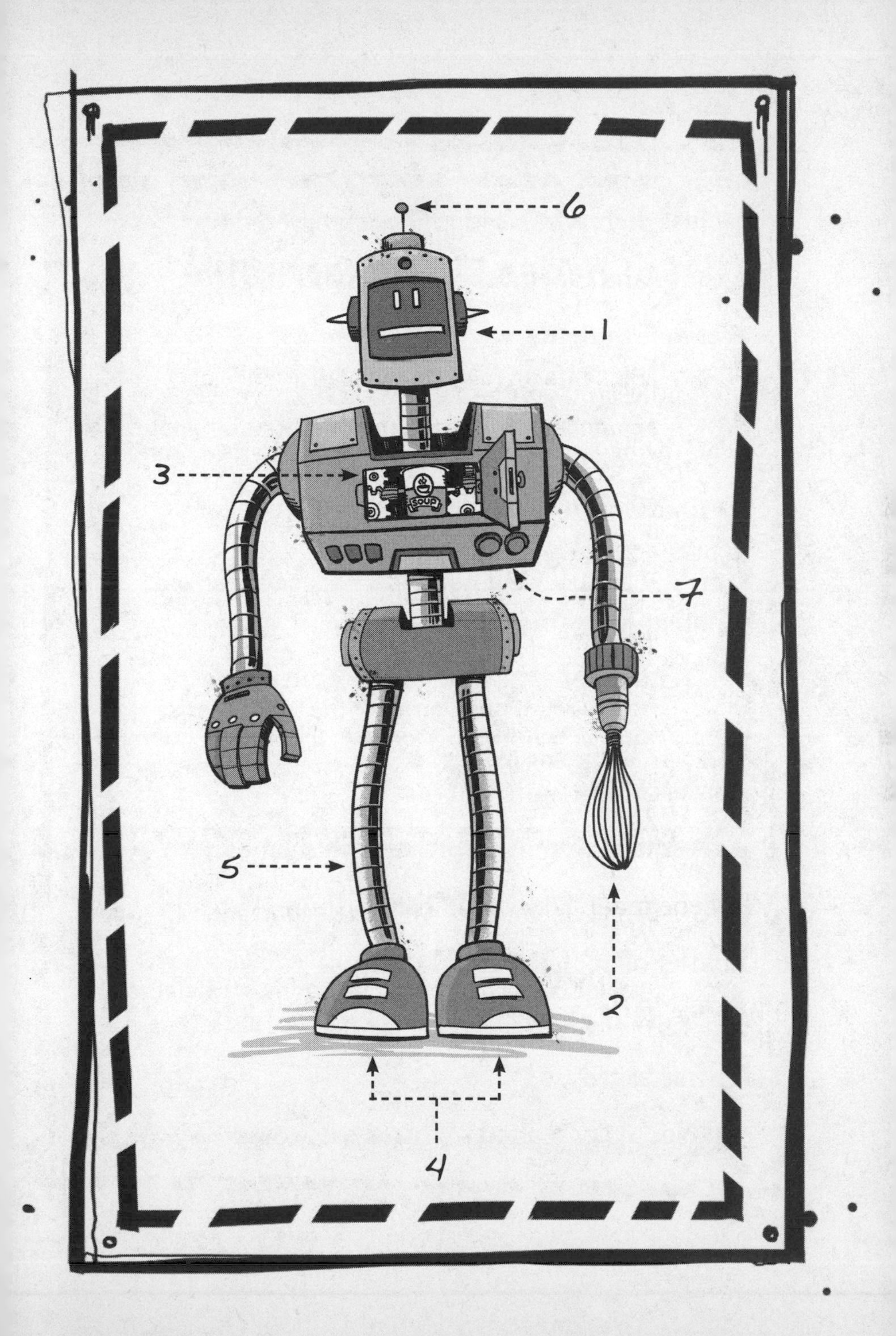
6
1
3
SOUP
7
5
2
4

Charles Character Profile

1. LED lights on face can display a range of emotions, from happy to not-quite-so-happy.
2. Whisk attachment. For whisking.
3. Thermonuclear power core housed in an old soup can.
4. Trendy robot sneakers, for the robot that's really going places.
5. Legs like metallic licorice laces.
6. Can't remember, but it looks important.
7. Deeply flawed and easily damaged artificial intelligence chip.

Create a Disaster Survival Kit

What would you put in your own Disaster Survival Kit?

Maybe, like Arty, a Bristly Brain Basher (aka toilet brush) is all you need to keep enemies at bay?

Can you invent a more sophisticated form of weaponry using a toilet roll or an empty cookie tin?

Or do you really just want some sweets and a clean T-shirt?

Pack your bag for the apocalypse and keep it by the door in case of disaster!

About the Author

R. McGeddon is absolutely sure the world is almost certainly going to end very soon. A strange, reclusive fellow—so reclusive, in fact, that no one has ever seen him, not even his mom—he plots his stories using letters cut from old newspapers and types them up on an encrypted typewriter. It's also believed that he goes by other names, including A. Pocalypse and N. Dov Days, but since no one has ever met him in real life, it's hard to say for sure. One thing we know is when the apocalypse comes, he'll be ready!